Dedication

This book is dedicated to all the young women and men that have been told they couldn't do something but did it anyways. It's people like you that do great things. A special thanks goes out to the many women like Kamala Harris, Michelle Obama, the U.S.A women's soccer team, Taylor Swift, Jessica Mendoza, and so many others that have served as inspirations. A special thanks also goes out to the many parents, coaches, and teachers who have served as an inspiration to others. Always remember no matter who you are -- young or old, male or female -- your inner strength is what guides you. Never let anyone else tell you are any less than who you are. Always be your own oak tree.

Editor: Jessica McLeod

Cover: Taylor Watkins

Back Photo: Rachel Yeomans

1

Summer Before 6th Grade

As I sit here and reminisce, I can't help but think about the years I spent growing up in Franklin and the people who influenced me along the way. Some of you may know me, while others of you may not. If you don't know who I am, that's okay. I am by no means insulted. My name is Calisa Hays, but most people know me as Cali.

I'm from the small rural town of Franklin which is found in southern Illinois a little more than two hours south of St. Louis. It's always been a rather quiet community. The area is mainly surrounded by farms, hills, and the Shawnee National Forest which blankets much of the region. It's always been a tight knit community. So closely knit that outsiders haven't always been welcomed. Over the years minorities have especially not been welcomed, which I witnessed and learned about as I got older. It wasn't just minorities. In all actuality, just about anyone who moved into the area had an uphill climb when it came to being accepted. The people of Franklin liked to gossip and get into each other's business.

I loved to play in the mud and run around with the other kids in the neighborhood, especially the boys, even though I was always picked last when teams were made. I guess it's because I was a girl. That didn't deter me at all though. In many ways it pissed me off and propelled me to try harder to prove them all wrong.

I'll never forget the time I asked a couple of the boys why I was picked last and one of the little punks responded, "because you're a girl, duh."

Talk about a gut punch!

Don't get me wrong. I would have loved to play with the girls, but the girls I knew seemed just a little to prissy for me.

Then one day my daddy, for whatever reason, decided to take me out golfing. It was a warm summer day. I was inside watching tv instead of running around outside with my friends. Probably because it was freaken hot out!

"Cali," he yelled from the garage with his booming voice. "Get your shoes on, we're going golfing."

Apparently he was ready to leave, with or without me, because his golf bag, which held all of his golf clubs, was slung over his shoulder.

I sprinted upstairs and within minutes I was down the stairs, out the door, and next to my dad's pickup. The last thing I wanted to do was upset him. Looking back I giggle because I didn't even ask him why he was inviting me or making me tag along. I just followed him like a sheep follows its herd. I do remember, however, sitting in the pickup seat and looking up at him in awe. I admired the hell out of my dad.

The trip to the golf course didn't take long at all. I leaped out of the truck. I was immediately awestruck at how green and colorful everything was. The flowers! The flowers were so pretty and rich with color!

My dad pulled out his bag of clubs from the back of his pickup and slung them over his shoulder.

At the time I thought that bag must have weighed 500 lbs or something goofy like that.

He looked at me and smiled.

"Come on Cali, let's go on inside the clubhouse."

On que, I sprinted after him. Heck, the last thing I wanted to do was get lost so I grabbed onto his right index finger with my left hand and I didn't dare let go.

I couldn't believe it. Everyone in the clubhouse knew him.

My dad is awesome, I thought to myself.

Not long after he paid at the front counter, a taller, older man walked in. He looked at me and smiled.

"JIM!" the tall man belted out with a smile across his face.

My dad turned around and noticed Don walk towards him.

"Hey you S.O.B!" My dad said with a laugh.

Of course, at the time I didn't quite know what S.O.B meant. S.O.B, what's S.O.B? Of course, I didn't dare ask my dad. Like a lot of things in life, that was one of those things I learned on my own.

Lost in thought, I didn't realize my dad was introducing

me to the man standing over me.

"Honey," he repeated, "you know Mr. Wilson."

Excited to be on this new adventure, I reached for his hand. "Hello sir," I said quietly in my 5th grade voice.

Don Wilson was a pretty cool guy. He was the varsity baseball coach and a science teacher at Franklin High School. My dad and he had coached together and had become good friends.

After Don paid for his round of golf, they gathered their bags and walked towards the door. Of course, I was an afterthought as they quickly approached the doors. My dad assumed I was behind them, which thankfully I was even though there were plenty of colors, shirts, golf balls, and other nic nacs to distract me.

As we pulled up in our golf carts to the first tee I looked around. I was mesmerized by the long green fields of short cut grass. As time went on I learned the tees were where the golfers started their hits or strokes. The sun, which nearly blinded me, glistened on the green grass and the leaves on the trees blew ever so lightly in the breeze. This was the beginning of my love affair with the game of golf.

2

Summer Before 6th Grade

A week after my big adventure to the golf course, my parents and I were at the dinner table eating pizza from Sammy's, the local pizza place.

My dad looked at my mom.

"Hun, Cali and I are going golfing tomorrow morning with Don."

Being the little 5th grader I was, I hung onto every word my dad said. Mom didn't say anything. My dad smiled and winked at me. Looking back, I wonder if they had already determined my fate for the next day. Either way, it didn't really matter because I enjoyed spending time with my dad. Heck, the last time he took me with him to the golf course I had a blast. He even bought me a hot dog, fries, and a soda afterwards which was pretty cool.

After woofing down the rest of my pizza, I scampered outside to play before the sun fell below the horizon. It wasn't long before my mom called me in for the night. Though I was slightly disappointed, overall it didn't matter. I knew the next day would be full of new experiences.

As excited as I was to be tagging along with my dad while he golfed, I had no idea he would wake me up at 6 a.m. That was not part of the original deal! I should admit, I would've been up sooner than later anyways.

I sluggishly put on my shorts and shirt laid out for me by my mom the night before and sauntered down the stairs. It's not like I was fully awake. To my surprise, dad and Mr. Wilson were sitting at the breakfast table drinking their cups of coffee. They were apparently waiting on me. I quickly learned rule number 1 -- be on time!

After having some buttered toast and juice they gathered their coffee containers. My dad also picked up a few juice drinks for me. I did everything I could to keep up with them. It was quite the challenge. Heck, one of their steps equaled two or three of mine.

The sun slowly appeared over the horizon. The grass was damp from the morning dew. We piled into Mr. Wilson's pickup. My dad and Mr. Wilson sat up front while I was relegated to the back. Heck, I nearly disappeared in the back seat since it was so big. I didn't care because I was on a new adventure with my dad.

Not long after they paid for their round of golf we appeared at the first tee. For those unsure, the tee is where you hit the ball for the first time at the beginning of each hole. Numerous times my dad glanced at me sternly and motioned for me to not talk while they were hitting their respective balls because it was proper etiquette. I was as quiet as a church mouse. The birds continued to chirp in the trees. Apparently they didn't get the memo.

I sat in the golf cart and watched my dad and Mr. Wilson yell at their golf balls after they hit it.

"Stay straight... stay straight... oh shit!"

"Come on baby, stay in...stay in."

"Nice!"

My favorite…"You're the man, nice one."

Other times they would yell at their clubs in agony after what they perceived was a bad shot.

Sometimes they quietly pumped their fists.

I was amazed how far they both hit the ball. I thought my dad was the strongest man in the world. After watching Mr. Wilson hit his ball, I concluded he was the second strongest man in the world. He hit the ball a long way also, but not as far as my dad. Heck, sometimes I lost track of the ball.

We whirled around the course in our carts, which was fun, until we finally reached the final hole. I was pooped and I didn't even hit the ball.

After we arrived home from our great adventure my dad and I went inside.

"Daddy," I blurted out, "I want to learn how to golf!"

"You do, huh?"

Before I had a chance to reply, he continued.

"I'll tell you what sweetie, if you're interested in it, we can get you a set of kid's clubs and let you hit the ball around here or at the driving range. Okay?"

In all honesty, that wasn't what I wanted to hear. No! I wanted to play with my dad on the golf course, but I knew there was no debating him. If I really wanted to play, this was the only option.

My dad knew I would pester him until we got those clubs. So immediately after lunch he took me to a sports store in Carbondale. Man was I excited! Christmas came early for me that year.

3

Spring 7th Grade

The next two years quickly sped by for me as I worked to improve my golf game. My dad would often take me to the driving range. Sometimes Mr. Wilson would join us, which I thoroughly enjoyed. Whether we went to the driving range in the morning or afternoon, a stop at the local donut shop was always an added bonus. The donuts were not necessarily the best, but they were donuts. I just enjoyed talking to my dad about school, golf, and life. It was our time. When Coach Wilson joined us he always had a fun story to share.

One day my teacher, Mr. Johnson, asked me why I golfed. Well of course, I loved the sport. The sound of the ball bouncing off my club, the challenge, and the time I got to spend with my dad were reasons enough.

I sat and looked at him, perplexed.

"I like golfing because it's fun," I answered eloquently.

"Huh," he responded, "well… It's just that you're a girl, which is why I'm asking."

I was in shock and a little pissed off.

"Well, my daddy takes me to the range several times a week and then we go for donuts afterwards," I responded with a smile. I mean, who doesn't like donuts?

Mr. Johnson couldn't seem to let it go. He was like a damn

dog with a bone!

"You do know it's a tough sport for girls, right?"

I was in no mood to argue with a middle aged fat guy who probably didn't have a clue about golf, so I did all I could to ignore him. Besides, I had happier things to think about. School was nearly done for the day and my dad had promised to take me out to the driving range once school was over.

Franklin was a relatively safe town to walk the streets in so I usually walked home after school as opposed to taking the school bus. I would walk on the sidewalk and imagine any number of scenarios. Some involved me saving the world from some terrible monster, while on other days I imagined hitting the shot of my life in some golf tournament with the crowd in the background chanting my name.

Soon after I arrived home, my dad pulled into the driveway. Even though I went to the same school where he worked, which was Franklin Middle School, I preferred not to wait on him when school was over. I think he preferred that as well. Surely the last thing he wanted was his little girl to be nagging him about going home for the day. Afterall, I did just that on the days I stayed and waited for him.

He smiled when he noticed me on the porch with my clubs by my side.

"You ready to go, hun?"

"Yah!"

I declared emphatically with a huge smile on my face as I jumped to my feet. I heaved my golf clubs over my shoulder and walked quickly to my dad's pickup.

He stood with his door open.

"Ah, I see. I guess I need to get my own clubs, eh?"

Truth be told, I wouldn't have been able to pick up his bag anyways. I think it weighed more than me! Imagine about 10 irons, 3 woods (which are the ones with a fatter club head than irons), a putter, several boxes of balls, and two towels. Plus the bag itself was big and bulky. I would've thought he could've stored a mini tv in that thing.

A minute later daddy emerged from the garage with his golf bag slung over his shoulder. When he reached the back of the truck he heaved his clubs, as well as mine, into the bed of the pickup. I sat patiently in the pickup and waited.

We finally arrived at the driving range. I loved going to the range right after school because there were generally fewer people there. While I waited for my dad at one of the tee boxes, I stretched my legs and back. Stretching wasn't something that came habitually to me. My dad forced me to stretch. There were times early on when he would emerge from the clubhouse and tell me to stretch. I would lie and tell him I had. He would smile or frown, depending on his mood, and point towards the clubhouse window.

"No, you didn't."

After several minutes of hitting golf balls, I stopped and looked at my dad.

"Dad, is it true I shouldn't play golf because I'm a girl?"

"Why do you ask that Cali?" he replied while he hit his ball.

"Well, Mr. Johnson told me today I shouldn't play golf because I'm a girl."

"Are you sure you didn't misunderstand him?"

I paused for a moment.

Before I had a chance to reply, my dad looked at me.

"Do you like to golf?"

"Yeah," I replied.

"Then who cares what he thinks. Prove him wrong." He paused. "You're going to run into people along the way who don't believe in you for one reason or another. If you believe in yourself, that's all that matters. Do you understand me?"

"Yes sir," I muttered.

For the next half hour I worked on my swing. From time to time my dad would stop and watch me.

Most times he would say "focus," "nice swing," or "you could do better."

Early on I had all kinds of challenges. I sometimes flat out wiffed when I swung. Other times I hit the ground several inches in front of the ball, which caused a chunk of dirt to go flying, while other times I hit the top of the ball with my club.

Thankfully, the more I practiced, the better I got.

Finally, after an hour, my dad looked at me.

"Okay Cali, do your sit-ups and push-ups. Then we can go."

At first I hated doing the push-ups and all, but the more times I did them the stronger and more defined my arms became, which I loved. I loved standing in front of the mirror and flexing. It gave me a sense of strength.

Though I wasn't ready to go home, I knew there would always be another day.

4

Spring 7th Grade

A couple of days after Mr. Johnson's lame discussion with me about women's inability to golf, I walked into Mr. Stamps' room. If I'm not mistaken, he had taught at Franklin middle school since the late 70s or early 80s. He had two grown daughters and he had a couple of granddaughters as well.

He was walking up and down the isles checking our work when he came to my desk. He looked at my work and smiled.

"Good job Cali, keep it up."

"Thanks!" I responded proudly.

He paused. "So how's golf going?"

I shrugged my shoulders.

"It's going well, sir. Been out at the driving range working on my swing quite a bit."

"Well that's awesome....You know my oldest daughter golfs with her husband quite a bit."

"No, I didn't know that."

"Well keep at it! Remember, it's like your work you do here. It's all about desire and preparation."

He moved on to the next student.

Lester, who was sitting behind me, tapped me on the shoulder. He was a scrawny kid. His blonde hair was always messed up which never matched the rest of his dress because he was always dressed half way decently. Especially for a seventh grader. I sometimes wondered if his mom dressed him. Not many kids wore collared shirts with khakis to school, but he sure did. ALL THE TIME!

"You golf?"

"Yeah, why?"

"Hmmm... that's interesting."

"Why's that interesting?"

" You're a girl. Girls should just stick to cleaning and other girly things."

"Excuse me?"

By now I was pissed. I wanted nothing more than to pop him in the jaw. I knew I could easily take him on, but he wasn't worth my energy nor was he worth a suspension.

"Well Lester, let me know when you want to lose in a game of golf."

He just looked at me with a goofy expression.

I turned around and ignored him the rest of the period. There was nothing more to say.

5

Summer Before 8th Grade

Several weeks later, my dad and I went to the driving range again. Only this time Mr. Wilson joined us. I liked it when he joined my dad and I because he always bought me a candy bar of one kind or another and a soda or a sports drink.

On our way home I overheard them discussing their plans to golf the next Saturday morning.

"Dad, can I join?" I asked enthusiastically!

Mr. Wilson looked back at me and smiled.

"What do you mean, 'can I come?' I figured you would be joining us already."

There was a pause.

"Make sure to bring your clubs," Mr. Wilson added.

I didn't immediately respond, though I did smile happily. I looked at my dad because I was unsure what to say.

My dad looked at me through the rear view mirror.

"He's serious, hun. You're joining us Saturday morning."

I continued to smile. I was so excited.

"Will you be able to get up for our 7 o'clock tee time though?" Mr. Wilson asked while smiling.

I think he knew the answer already.

"Uh, yeah!" I replied enthusiastically.

Two days later I awoke to my alarm blaring Taylor Swift's

You Belong With Me. The morning sun was still hiding below the horizon. I gracefully rolled myself out of bed -- if there was such a way. The light from the hallway appeared from underneath my bedroom door. I could hear my dad fixing breakfast in the kitchen. Thankfully, I had laid my clothes out the previous night, a practice that would come in handy down the road. I staggered to the dresser and grabbed my shorts and t-shirt. Waking up at 5:30 in the morning didn't even cross my mind as crazy. Instead, I was excited to be playing golf on a real golf course with my dad and Mr. Wilson.

After several minutes of piddle paddling, I joined my dad for some morning eggs, toast, and juice. These were the times I really enjoyed spending time with my dad. In retrospect, I wish I had spent more times like these with my dad.

Finally, after nearly 20 minutes, we heard a knock at the back door. My dad turned and smiled.

"Well, good morning, Coach."

A cool gush of air followed him when he opened the door.

Some people are good at whispering while others aren't. Mr. Wilson's whisper voice wasn't the best so when he said, "Hey guys," it nearly sounded like he was using a megaphone.

Like the innocent little youngster I was, I just sat in my chair and smiled as I chewed my buttered toast. After my dad and Mr. Wilson greeted each other, they looked at me impatiently. The last thing I wanted to do was start off on the wrong foot again, so I wolfed down the final bites of my toast and gulped down the last few drops of my cranberry juice.

We piled into my dad's pickup with me in the back, which I really didn't mind so much. I was actually surprised how empty the parking lot was when we arrived at the course. I figured it would be full of people like us wanting to hit the course, or as my dad liked to call them -- "the links." It was cool to see the sun rise over the horizon and even neater to see the dew glisten on the grass. Thankfully the shoes I was wearing didn't soak in the morning dew from the ground. Otherwise, my socks would've been drenched by the sixth hole. After they paid, they peeled around to the front of the clubhouse in two separate golf carts. I waited for them patiently by the pickup.

We loaded the golf bags onto the golf carts and sped towards the first hole. Of course, I use the word "sped," loosely. We were in golf carts afterall and they aren't the fastest vehicles.

I began to shake with excitement as we approached the first hole. Even though I had golfed at one of the smaller courses, this was my first time on a real full-fledged golf course. The carts rolled to a stop at the first hole. My dad and I were in one of the carts while Mr. Wilson scooted around on the other one.

My dad looked at me assertively.

"You stay here while we hit our shots. Now, remember, don't say a word while we're hitting, okay?"

Of course I didn't want to ruin my chance to play golf with my dad, so I nodded my head like the good daughter I was. They walked up to the tee box with their drivers in hand. For you non golfers out there, the driver is the biggest club, which is used for hitting the ball off the tee. My dad looked at Mr. Wilson and then pointed to the tee box. Mr. Wilson nodded and smiled. He stepped up and put his tee in the ground. His ball sat upon the top of the tee like a cherry on a sundae. I sat in wonderment. Mr. Wilson took two practice swings in an attempt to loosen up his body. The third time he stepped up, lined up his feet, wiggled his club, and with a giant backswing --

WHACK!

His ball flew off the tee like a guided missile, eventually landing some 250 yards down the middle of the fairway. From his reaction I could tell the ball landed exactly where he wanted it to land. I sat in the golf cart amazed at what I just saw.

As if my dad copied Mr. Wilson, he stepped up and took several practice swings.

WHACK!

His ball flew off the tee as well and landed about fifteen feet from Mr. Wilson's ball in the middle of the fairway.

Next up, me!

My dad jumped in the golf cart and sped us down the cart path towards the ladies' tee approximately 75 yards in front of the men's tee boxes. It took me a while to understand why women's tees were farther up. Apparently we can't hit the ball as far. He stopped beside the ladies' tees and looked at me.

"Show us what you got."

"Yes sir," I said nervously.

I think my dad knew I was a little nervous.

"Have fun, Cali. Show us what you got," he repeated confidently.

We walked towards the middle of the tee box which was marked by these two big large white looking golf balls. He bent over and put the tee into the ground with the ball on top of the tee.

Confidently, I stepped up to the ball, set my feet, looked down the middle of the fairway, and then took two practice swings. After taking a deep breath I raised my club in my back swing and swung as hard as I could.

TING!

I looked up and watched my ball fly down the middle of the fairway. Excited, I turned and looked at my dad. He had a huge smile on his face. Both Mr. Wilson and my dad clapped their hands and cheered as my ball came to a slow stop about 150 yards away from me in the middle of the fairway.

I was hooked!

6

Summer Before 8th Grade

A week after my golf outing with my dad and Mr. Wilson, my parents and I were having dinner. It was one of those typical summer Friday evenings. I could hear the crickets in the distance as I chomped away on my pizza.

"Cali, you want to go golfing Sunday with Mr. Wilson and I?"

I looked at him with my mouth open as if he was on crack or something.

"Of course I want to go!" I exclaimed.

My dad smiled.

"Good."

After I finished my supper, I ran outside to the garage. I dragged my bag out of the garage and laid it down. I dug through it seperating the good balls from the bad ones. After separating the good balls from the bad ones, I began to count the good ones. Next, I unzipped one of the side pockets and pulled out my tees and other trinkets. I wanted to make sure I was well prepared for Sunday.

After I did my bag check, I gleefully dragged my bag back into the garage. I made a note to myself to remind my dad I needed more good balls. Otherwise, I was set.

Finally, Sunday arrived. That morning when I woke up I

could hear thunder in the distance, but that didn't stop us from loading up the truck for what was becoming our weekly trip to the golf course.

"Damn... look at that lighting," my dad muttered.

Way off in the distance we could see several flashes of lightning.

"Yeah, let's keep our fingers crossed," Mr. Wilson replied as thunder rumbled in the distance.

Of course, at the time, I didn't fully understand the science of swinging a metal club around with lightning in the area. Apparently you don't want to wave a golf club in the air like a magic wand.

We arrived at the golf course, unloaded the truck, paid, and then headed towards the first tee box. In the distance, the sun was blanketed by the dark clouds. As I stood on the first tee I looked out towards the pristine fairways in front of me. I was awestruck by the orange colored clouds in the distance.

We made it through the first few holes without any problems. The whole time my Dad and Coach looked for lightning. A light drizzle did fall on us from the start, but it was nothing to keep us from golfing.

At one point my dad sternly looked at me.

"If you see any lightning, tell Mr. Wilson or I."

We approached the fifth hole when the skies became really dark. We were on top of a hill which overlooked the fairway. In the distance, on the edge of the fairway, stood a huge oak tree which must have been one hundred years old. The rain began to slowly pick up. Suddenly, out of nowhere, lightning shook us and the hairs on my arms stood up.

Coach looked at my dad and then me. They immediately jumped into their individual golf carts. Of course, new to this kind of thing, it took me a little longer, but I quickly realized I needed to join my dad in the golf cart.

As soon as I jumped in, we zoomed towards the clubhouse. The rain hit us from all sides. It was coming down so hard it actually stung! Finally, we reached the clubhouse.

Coach Wilson was the last one in the building when several loud claps of thunder boomed overhead, followed by several flashes of lightning. The lights flickered as the storm roared through. In the distance I even heard the tornado siren whir erily. Frantically, we ran to the lower level. This, of course, totally freaked me out since this had never happened to me before.

Finally, after what seemed to be an eternity, the sirens came to a stop. Not long after, the rain slowed to a light drizzle and we all moved to the ground floor. I longingly looked out the window and determined our day on the golf course was done.

My dad looked at me and then Coach Wilson.

"Coach, what do you think?"

Don looked at my dad.

"Well, it may be a little wet out there, but what do we have to lose?"

I remember him finishing the sentence with a huge smile.

Don curiously looked at me.

"What do you think, Cali? Should we continue?"

Of course, I was just glad to be along for the ride. If it meant getting a little wet, then so be it. We were wet already after all. We zipped back down the path from where we came. My dad slowed the cart to an eventual stop. We all looked to our left. My mouth was as wide as a canyon. I couldn't believe what I was looking at. The huge oak tree, which struck me before because of its beauty and size, was lying sadly on the ground.

My dad slumped his shoulders. He looked at both Don and I.

"Huh, that large clap we heard must have caused this. Don, what do you think?"

"Yep, must have been that," he replied confidently.

I looked at the tree and thought it was a sad sight to see. It was too bad such a beautiful tree couldn't survive the storm. I lost my mood to golf. Why? I couldn't explain it.

Well, my golf score took a mighty turn for the worst after the discovery of the oak tree, but then again the wet soggy grass surely didn't help matters either. We eventually finished the round and had some juice and a donut in the clubhouse. The rain had cleared and the day was shaping up to be a nice one, but sadly that beautiful oak tree didn't make it.

7

Summer Before 8th Grade

My 8th grade year was fast approaching and summer was quickly coming to a close. My mom and dad, along with Coach and his wife, decided to get together one final time for steaks. My dad and Don both loved to grill out whenever they could. Most of the time we got together with the intention of eating around six, but my dad and Coach Wilson apparently had other ideas. All too often they'd stand over the grill with a beer in their hands and talk. For whatever reason, what should've taken thirty minutes often turned into a two to three hour affair.

I didn't seem to mind. They let me sit outside and listen to their conversations while I sipped on my soda. As they told their stories, they'd sprinkle in a swear word or two as if I wasn't there.

They were no more than thirty minutes into their grilling adventure when Coach looked at my dad.

"Get this, we have two players moving into the community from Aurora."

My dad looked at Coach, intrigued.

"Yeah, I guess the oldest is a pretty good pitcher. Apparently he's just a junior. His former coach even called me today. I guess he throws the ball in the mid 90s. And get this,

his younger brother is only a freshman and he catches, which is a position we'll need this year."

There was a pause in the conversation. My dad listened intently. I pretended to be doing something else, but they knew full well I was listening. I'm sure of it.

Coach continued.

"They sound like great kids and athletes. There's just one hitch. I mean, it won't bother me, but I'm sure some of the people in this town will get their underwear in a bundle."

"Yeah, what's that?" my dad asked when Coach paused.

"Well...they're black, and you know how this town is when it comes to blacks. Yeah, it shall be interesting."

I could sense a bit of disdain in his voice.

In my head, I wondered what the problem was. They were black, so what?! Then I began to count the number of African Americans who went to our school or lived in Franklin. The number was, of course, zero. In my ever curious young teenage mind, I began to wonder why that was.

"Dad, why don't blacks live here?"

My dad paused. He was always quite calculated in the way he spoke and I could tell he was running the answer through his head.

"Well Cali, that's just the way it has always been for whatever reason. It's not right, but then again, there are a lot of things in this world which aren't right."

Of course I had all kinds of questions in my head, but I determined this was not the time or place to ask. I mean, don't take me wrong -- both my dad and Don are great guys, but I think they were more interested in drinking their beers and telling stories than answering some questions from an inquisitive 8th grader. So, I just sat quietly in my chair and sipped my soda.

As the two continued grilling the steaks, they talked more baseball. I could tell Don was excited about his future team. I could also tell he was concerned with how the team might react to the move-ins.

The evening eventually came to a close and school was just a few weeks away. This wasn't the last I heard about Julio and Jeremy. Though school was about to begin and summer was coming to a close, I still found time to golf.

8

Summer Before 8th Grade

School was only two weeks away and I was far from ready. One evening I was up in my room reading a cool story about some prince when I heard a knock on my bedroom door. To my surprise, it was my dad. He didn't normally bother me during my alone time. With a newspaper in hand, he approached my bed and sat down.

"How would you like to enter a teen golf tournament in Carbondale a few weeks from now?"

I could tell by the smile on his face and the gleam in his eyes that he wanted me to say yes.

At the time, I didn't truly appreciate my talents yet. I loved golf, but I didn't think I was that good. I probably thought I wasn't that good because I was a girl and I had a lot of self-doubt.

"Do you think I'm good enough?"

"Cali, it doesn't matter if you're good or not. Do you enjoy golfing?"

"Yes," I quickly responded.

"Then let's sign you up and see how you do. I'll be your caddy. How does that sound?"

He should have started off with that statement. As soon as he said he would be my caddy, I was sold. I nodded my head enthusiastically.

Several weeks later, the golf tournament finally arrived. This was a new experience for me, so I didn't know what to expect. I was in the 6th graders through 8th graders age group.

After we signed in, my dad took me to the driving range so I could hit some practice balls. I was glad my dad refrained from commenting a whole lot. I was already nervous. I didn't need him to make it worse by commenting on every little thing. When he did comment, he would remind me of my hips, wrists, proper breathing, or some other key point in my swing.

I have to admit, while I practiced I looked around at the competition. I kept thinking to myself, *I am better than her, oh geez I'm definitely better than her* along with other opinions I won't mention here. That is when I first came to the realization that I really wasn't that bad of a golfer.

While I set myself up for a practice putt, my dad tapped me on my left shoulder. For those unsure what putting is, it's when you are up on the green which is the real short grass, and you're trying to tap the ball into the little hole. It's tougher than it looks.

"Time to take on the rest of the field." he said with a smile.

Up to that point I was fairly calm and relaxed. That quickly changed. I was so glad I wasn't the first one to hit in my group. The first girl stepped up into the tee box to hit her ball. She went through her practice swings which I thought were decent enough. Finally, she stepped up to the ball and set her feet. She went into her backswing and moved forward with her swing.

CHUNK!

The poor girl hit the ground in front of the ball with her club head. The ball came to a stop ten yards in front of her while a chunk of grass and dirt went flying. Her second hit, which was a penalty shot, went much better, but it sure made things easier on me watching her struggle.

I confidently stepped up to the tee. I went through my routine like I had done hundreds of times before. The only difference, those times were not in a competition. After taking one more glance down the fairway, I swung like there was no tomorrow.

Phew!

I was so happy when the ball flew off the tee and landed 125 yards away from me. It eventually came to a stop in the middle of the fairway. I looked at my dad and smiled. I was so proud of myself. He pumped his fist several times. Yeah, my dad was pretty excited for me.

Well all things considered, my first tournament went

alright. I didn't win, but I did do rather well, especially considering this was "my first rodeo."

My dad and I were on our way home the second day after chasing my little white ball around the golf course. The air conditioner in the pickup sure felt good because we were both dripping with sweat from the August heat.

"Dad, when can I do this again?"

I looked at him with a smile. If he wasn't persuaded already, I thought my smile would hopefully convince him.

"So you want to do this again, huh?"

"Yep," I replied enthusiastically.

"Well then, we'll do this again. You did a good job out there, especially for only playing a few years. I'm proud of you."

Looking back, I can't help but thank my dad. He had a nice way of encouraging me.

9

Fall 8th Grade

My 8th grade began uneventfully, which was the way I liked it. I never really was into school even though I did well, behaved, and pretended to like my classes. Every few days my dad took me out to the driving range so I could practice. Gradually I improved, which kept me motivated.

One day in late fall, a girl I recognized from school came out to the driving range with her dad. At the time I didn't think much about it, but it soon became apparent I wasn't the only girl in Franklin that golfed.

Carley was a 7th grader -- one grade lower than me. She was originally from Kentucky and moved to Franklin her 6th grade year. At the time, I wondered why in the world someone would move here to Franklin. I mean this was just a small country town. If you wanted to do anything you'd have to drive to Carbondale. Don't get me wrong, a small town like Franklin had it's merits when you're a little kid. That you didn't have to rely on your parents when you wanted to play with your friends was probably the best quality.

Carley and her dad walked up with a bucket of balls and set their bucket down a few spots down from me. Eventually my dad started talking to her dad. I tried not to eavesdrop, but let's be honest, I was curious what they were talking about.

The next thing I knew, my dad had arranged a golf outing with Carley and her dad. Heck, if it meant me golfing, I was all in. I also began to notice her around school more, probably because I had a face to go by. She seemed very quiet, but genuine. In a small town like Franklin where everyone knows everyone, the genuine people usually rise to the top like cream, while the not so genuine people gossip about them.

Eventually the week came to a close and Friday turned into Saturday. With fall around the corner, the temperature began to slowly cool. Because of the cooler temperatures, we didn't schedule our golf outing as early as my dad and Don liked, but it was early enough. I didn't really care when we started, I just wanted to golf no matter what time of day it was.

My dad hit the first tee shot followed by Carley's Dad. Once they hit, they drove us down to our tee spots. I looked at Carley.

"You wanna hit first?"

She just shrugged her shoulders. She had a quiet demeanor about her.

"Go ahead and hit," I said with a smile.

She stepped up and set her ball on her tee. She took a few practice swings and SWOOSH!

Her ball bounced off her tee like a laser.

I looked at her ball and then her.

"Nice shot."

"Thanks," she replied with a smile.

As we worked our way through the golf course, I was quite impressed with ole Carley. Man she could hit the ball. She was constantly hitting the ball into the middle of the fairway. I knew I was good, but she was equally as good.

Carley and I were walking side by side as we approached the eighteenth hole. I could hear the birds sing around us.

"Look Carley, our balls are next to each other on the green."

"Yeah I see that," she replied nonchalantly.

We both looked around, but couldn't see either one of our dad's balls.

"Hey dad!" Carley yelled. "Where's your ball? Both Cali's and mine are up on the green."

We both giggled.

"Yeah, yeah, yeah," replied Carley's dad.

Just before our dad's tapped their balls onto the green, I looked at Carley. She looked at me in return and grinned.

"I enjoyed playing with you." I said.

She nodded her head. "Thanks, so did I."

Even though she was fairly quiet, I really enjoyed playing with her. Her dad was a nice guy and quite the golfer like my dad, though my dad did hit the ball farther than him.

Later that afternoon, I was up in my room fiddling with my computer and pretending to be working on my homework when I heard a knock at the door. Before I had a chance to respond, my dad slowly walked through the door and sat down at the foot of my bed. He looked at me with a proud smile. At the time I didn't fully appreciate those looks. I thought he was weird.

"Did you have fun this morning golfing with Carley?"

"Truth be told, I think I would have enjoyed golfing with anyone, but yeah. She was fun."

"Well, would you be game to go golfing with her and her dad again?"

I shrugged my shoulders. Even though I enjoyed golfing with my dad and Don a lot more, it was nice to golf with someone my age. I don't think it really would have mattered if I had said "no" anyways.

A few weeks later we all went golfing again. The temperatures were definitely cooler, so we, thankfully, golfed later in the day. The funny thing is, neither Carley nor I seemed overly competitive, but you put a little white ball down in front of us and we both flipped on a dime, especially the more we played against each other.

One of the best examples of this was when we were on the 7th hole. She nailed, I mean *nailed*, a shot down the middle of the fair.

I stepped up and hit my ball hard, but it drifted towards a couple of the larger oak trees to the right of the fairway. In frustration, I slammed my club into the ground.

"Too bad," she said.

I know she didn't mean anything by it, but I wasn't happy. Probably more so about my ball than what she said.

Well, a few holes later the tables had turned. We were approaching the 11th hole when Carley had one of the worst shots I had ever seen.

"Oh shit!" she bellowed.

"Carley!" I replied.

She looked at me rather sternly.

"You're not my dad. I can swear if I want. Especially when I hit a bad shot." She mumbled just loud enough for me to hear.

Yep, we weren't the same lovable girls once we stepped onto that golf course.

Most of the time though, we were supportive of each other. I can't speak for Carley's dad, but I think my dad thought it was good for me to compete with someone my age. In retrospect, it was good preparation.

Even though we pretended not to keep score, I did in my head. Let me tell you, I was glad I beat her. I didn't win by much. She was, afterall, pretty damn good.

Our school was small enough that the 7th and 8th graders all ate at the same time. Even though we were a grade apart, as time passed, she and I sat next to each other more and more.

It was kind of nice. Not many of my friends understood the golfing thing. Most students just looked at me and wondered why I, a girl, was out there anyways.

10

Winter 8th Grade

Christmas finally arrived my 8th grade year. That meant I didn't have school and golf season was only a few months away. Carley and I also began to hang out more.

It was the first Friday of our Christmas break. Carley and I persuaded our parents to let her stay the night. We were up in my room relaxing as dinner time approached. It was Friday, which meant my parents would either take us out for pizza or they would order in.

I rolled over and looked at Carley, who was enamored with the movie we had on.

"So how long have you been golfing?"

Several seconds passed before she looked at me.

"What?"

"How long have you been golfing?" I asked again.

"Oh sorry...I've been golfing since the fourth or fifth grade. What about you?"

I looked at the ceiling as I went back in time.

"I guess it was fifth grade for me."

"I like golfing but don't love it." she added.

"Then why do you golf?"

She shrugged her shoulders.

"I guess because my dad wants me to and I'm good at it.

It's the one thing he seems to approve of. Sometimes I don't feel like I can do much right." She paused. "Sometimes I think he wishes I was a boy."

"Dinner!" my mom yelled from the kitchen. Abruptly, our golf conversation came to an end, but it stuck with me.

A couple days later Christmas arrived, which meant dinner with Don and his wife. Since my 6th grade year, we alternated between their place and ours. Since they didn't have any kids or family in the area, I had become the beneficiary.

For the record, I had no issues with the additional gifts and attention.

After dinner -- which consisted of ham, dressing, green beans, sweet potatoes and bread -- we marched into the living room. I, of course, would always join because I loved listening to the stories they would share. Especially if the stories came from Coach Wilson. He could be quite the storyteller.

"So Don, how's the team going to be this year?" my dad asked.

Don smiled.

I learned early on if you wanted to make Mr. Wilson smile, baseball was always a good way to do it.

"Well, we should be alright. Of course you never know with injuries and eligibility, but I think we should be decent."

"How are those two young men you were talking about this summer doing? Are they going to be any good?" my dad asked.

A silence swept through the room.

His wife chimed in.

"Oh man, he won't stop talking about those two! Especially the oldest one."

"Oh yeah, how so?" I asked, jumping into the conversation.

"Well, let's just say Julio, he's the oldest of the two, has the ability to go pro and his younger brother looks talented."

"He throws hard, does he?" my dad asked.

"Ohhh yeah. I have seen him throw in the gym. This kid can bring it. You guys are going to have to come out and see a game this spring when he's pitching."

I looked at my dad enthusiastically. That would be exciting. In my eyes as a junior high student, high school was such a big deal. At least it was for me.

"So how are the other kids treating them?" my dad asked.

I sat there perplexed. I didn't understand the question. They were high schoolers. I thought, *why wouldn't they be treated alright?*

"Well sadly, that's a whole different story. It's been a struggle for them. Many of the kids have not been very welcoming. I don't see them welcoming them until baseball starts and hopefully they will see how good they are."

Still a little perplexed, I couldn't help but ask.

"Why? What's the problem with them?"

Don looked at me. I looked at my dad who sat in his big chair silently as if someone pressed his mute button.

"They're black, Cali," Coach added.

"I don't get it. What's wrong with that?" I asked innocently.

"Sweetie, remember, we talked about this this past summer. This town hasn't been the most welcoming to minorities," my dad added.

"Well I think that's stupid!" I declared adamantly.

Everyone in the room laughed.

"Well time will tell, but I will say they're talented. I hope they don't leave this place." Coach took a sip of his drink and paused. He looked at me. I think he was ready to change the subject.

"So how's golf going?"

Whenever someone asked me about golf I would smile. Unlike Carley, I loved talking about the game I loved. I shook my head enthusiastically.

"It's going well! I'm getting better."

"Well, don't forget about us when you make it big, Cali." he added with a smile.

The night came to a close. It was always fun to sit around and listen to the grownups talk, but the end of the evening had to come. On a positive note, we were one step closer to spring, which meant more golfing.

11

Spring 8th Grade

After some time away from the golf course because of winter, my dad and I began to hit the driving range again. Trust me, I was ready to get back out there. There was only so much I could do in my house. I wasn't much of a bookworm, even though I did well in school. I did have Carley to hang out with, but she was a year younger than me.

One afternoon in late March, I remember swinging away at the driving range. For some reason I was getting quite frustrated. Maybe because the cold wind was blowing in my face, or maybe it was because my nose was runny. Who the hell knows. I do know I wasn't hitting the ball particularly well.

My dad looked at me.

"Hey Cali,"

"What!?"

I didn't mean to sound bitchy, but I know I did.

My dad opened his mouth then paused. He waited a few seconds.

"Relax. You're swinging with a temperament."

Though his words weren't that comforting for this 8th grader, I still acknowledged him.

"Yes sir."

I took a deep breath and stepped up to my next ball. Low

and behold I hit that son of gun 150 yards. I know that doesn't seem like much, but it was into the wind. I put another ball up on the tee and swung away.

TING!

That one flew 150 yards away as well. I looked at my dad and grinned.

He smiled back.

"See, I told you."

"Yes sir."

I had a huge grin on my face.

After about thirty minutes of gleeful swinging, my dad stopped and looked at me. It was not uncommon for him to stop what he was doing and watch me for a few minutes. I think this was his excuse to spend time with me.

"Cali, how would you like to go for a donut?"

What?! A donut?! I wasn't going to pass that up!

"Sure," I declared gleefully.

"Well, before we go you have to get your pushups in."

"Ugg..." I groaned as I got down on my hands and knees.

My dad totally knew how to sucker me in. Dangle a donut in front of me and I would gladly do my pushups!

Franklin wasn't a very big town, so it didn't take long for us to reach our destination. We sat quietly in the donut shop. I got my favorite chocolate glazed donut and milk. My dad ordered his typical cinnamon roll and coffee. I remember to this day the glee he had as he sat down at the table with his roll and coffee. Again, I thought it was all about me. I think he would have found a way to get himself that afternoon treat had I not done what he asked.

After a few minutes of quiet, my dad put down his cup of black coffee. Yes, black coffee. As disgusting as it sounds, he liked it.

"So, how would you like to go to a baseball game in a few weeks to see this new pitcher Don was talking about?"

I sat up enthusiastically. I always loved baseball. Since I was a girl, I was never allowed to play baseball and softball never interested me for some reason.

"Can we!?" I asked with youthful enthusiasm.

"Of course we can. I'll ask Don when he thinks we should go. Alright?"

I chomped away at my donut, not really knowing or comprehending the fact that I was going to get to see a future major leaguer in action. I was just excited to go watch a high school baseball game.

12

Spring 8th Grade

My dad and I came upon the Franklin High School ball field. I can't remember who they were playing that day, but I remember being mesmerized by the number of fans. I thought it was the coolest thing! We sat at the far end of the bleachers. Many of the students looked so big, even though I was actually taller than some of them. I must have looked like a little kid at an amusement park. I was so excited! Eventually, the ball team came out of the dugout in their blue uniforms. It was pretty cool to see.

I was distracted until I felt an elbow in my side.

"Look Cali, there's the player Coach was telling us about."

I looked towards the dugout. Standing by himself was a giant. I watched him move around as if he was deep in thought, only to have another player walk up beside him. The other player was a few inches smaller, not built nearly as big, and draped in catcher's gear. I figured they must have been brothers since they were the only two black kids on the team.

"That must be his brother," my dad added.

I just nodded my head.

Finally, the Franklin High School team took the field. On top of the mound was the player we had come to see.

"Dad, what's his name?"

He looked at the two students, who sat behind us.

"Excuse me, can you tell me what the pitcher's name is?"

Interestingly enough, the two students looked at my dad as if he had four eyes or something. I thought it was a simple enough question, but apparently they didn't think so.

Begrudgingly, one of the students answered my dad.

"His name is Julio, sir. He's new here."

My dad looked at me and smiled after nudging me in the side.

"I guess they woke up on the wrong side of the bed or had a bad day at school."

Of course that made me giggle.

"Did you hear them? His name is Julio." he repeated.

I nodded my head again and smiled.

I was simply in awe of Julio's stature. He just looked like a beast standing on top of the mound and I mean that in the most complimentary way. The first few warm up pitches wizzed towards home plate. His brother, Jeremy, was behind home plate receiving the pitches. Though athletic looking, he was nothing like his brother in height or size.

I looked over at my dad who was entranced at the game in front of him. He had always been a sports fan, but I never really knew how much he loved baseball. I guess he just never made it obvious, or he was just careful never to alienate me, which meant a lot if that happened to be the case.

"Wow, Cali, These guys are pretty good," he said with a happy smile at one point.

As the game finished up, my dad and I sat on the bleachers quietly. I've always been the type to watch people, so it didn't bother me. The players lined up and shook hands with the opposing team. Interestingly, not one of the Franklin players gave Julio or his brother, Jeremy, any high fives or recognition. If they did, it wasn't obvious. Julio was, after all, the winning pitcher and Jeremy caught a hell of a game.

I looked at my dad.

"Why aren't the players praising Julio or his brother?"

"Some people are just that way, dear." he replied.

He paused.

"Promise me you'll never be like that."

"Yes sir."

There was another pause.

"Are you ready to go, Cali?"

I nodded my head without muttering a word. I was ready to get home.

My dad put his arm around me and smiled.

"Come on, sweetie. Let's get home and have some dinner. I'm sure your mom will be glad to see us."

13

Spring 8th Grade

After some discussion, my dad signed me up for another golf tournament. This one was in the St. Louis area. As the tournament approached, I went out to the driving range almost every day to prepare. The two best parts about my semi-daily practices were the time I spent with my dad and the improvement I could see myself making.

The Friday before the tournament, I piled into the pickup with my dad. Mom was never much of a golf fan and she knew the time spent with my dad was important, so she stayed behind and held down the fort.

The drive was about two to two and half hours. Much of the drive was on two lane highways that wound alongside the Mississippi, which was quite relaxing.

I continued to stare out the window after a brief nap.

"Dad? Is Carley signed up for this tournament?"

"I don't know honey...why?"

I shrugged my shoulders.

"I don't know. It's always nice to know someone at one of these things I guess."

"Well you know me," he replied sarcastically.

I sat silent in my seat for a minute or two.

"That doesn't even deserve a reply," I replied.

After we checked into the hotel room, we went for pizza. We still had to have pizza even though we were in a different town.

We sat in the booth silently eating.

"You're quiet sweetie. Everything okay?"

"Yeah, I'm just tired."

I didn't want to tell him, but I was slightly nervous. Thankfully, I had a supportive dad.

After we devoured our pepperoni pizza, we walked quietly back to the hotel. The room wasn't much, but we weren't going to spend much time in it the next few days anyways. The bed was comfortable enough which was all that really mattered.

As soon as I walked through the bedroom door, I claimed my bed and laid down. My dad sat on the bed next to mine.

"Hey Cali, you mind if I watch a little TV?"

I prodded my eyes open for a quick second and smiled.

"Nope."

What seemed like fifteen minutes must have been several hours. Even though the lights were off in the room, the TV was still on.

I looked to my left towards my dad.

"Dad?"

No reply.

"Dad?" I asked again softly.

A loud snore boomed across the room.

Yep, he was asleep. I peeled myself off my bed and tiptoed towards the TV. After fumbling for the off button, the room went black. I immediately realized that was a big mistake. I just hoped I wouldn't stub my toe.

The next morning, I rolled over and looked at the time. It was way too early. I looked across the room and heard my dad. If I wasn't mistaken, I would have thought a lumberjack was in my room cutting down the biggest oak tree.

Restlessly, I laid in my bed and waited for my dad to wake up. I was ready to get the day started.

After lying in bed for what seemed to be eternity, my dad finally woke up, stretched, and looked in my direction. Our eyes met. I gave him the biggest grin.

"Well, good morning, Cali. Are you ready to get your golf on?" he asked with a tired smirk.

Excitedly, I shook my head. "Yes!"

It was only 6:30 and my tee time wasn't until 9. That didn't matter. I was ready to get up and get going. It's not like I was going to fall asleep. I just needed the green light from my dad. I didn't want to wake him up after all. He stretched a few more times, but I didn't wait for him. I jumped out of bed and ran into the bathroom for my shower. Though the shower was more of a quick spritz, it served its purpose. It's not like I was going to smell like roses after a day of golf, but I didn't want to stink at the first tee. I jumped out of the shower, dried off, threw on some sweats, and briskly walked out of the bathroom towards my bed.

I laid out my outfit the night before. I was far from a fashionista, but my mom bought me the cutest pink collared shirt to go with the cutest pair of pants. I have to admit, at the time, I thought I was the bomb.

My dad didn't take long to get ready. By 7:30 we were out of the room and heading towards the lobby. We always had to stay at a place that served continental breakfast. It was non-negotiable with my dad, which was fine by me. At the time I thought it was kind of corny, but once I started to travel on my own, I appreciated those continental breakfasts.

After our small breakfast, dad drove us to the golf course. The temperature was delightfully pleasant with just enough sun to get me burnt. Thankfully, I did wear sunscreen.

My dad pulled my clubs out from the back of the pickup.

"Why don't you go get some swings in and I'll register you."

I was in no mood to practice, but I knew better than to question my dad.

"Yes sir." I muttered.

After several swings on the driving range and a few practice putts on the practice green, I put my putter into my golf bag. I had worked up a minor sweat, so I wiped the sweat off my face with my towel, which was resting on my bag. After wiping my face, I took a deep breath and threw my towel over my shoulder.

"You ready to rock, hun?"

I stuck out my fist for him to hit.

After a soft fist bump, we slowly walked towards the first tee box. I thought back to my first tournament and remembered the girl who chunked her first tee shot. It made me giggle. I needed to relax some because the number of fans at the first tee box was overwhelming. Then again, any fans more than five would have impressed me.

I was to hit last in my group, which was fine with me. I wanted to see what my competition was like. The first two girls stepped up to their balls respectively and took a good whack, though there wasn't much to show for it. I'll give them points for trying, but their balls didn't fly very far. The third girl did a little better, but not by much. I watched her ball fly a little over a hundred yards and then drop in the middle of the fair way. Slightly nervous, I looked at my dad and took a deep breath.

"You got this," he whispered.

I didn't reply. Instead, I walked towards the middle of the tee box and teed my ball up. I stepped back behind my ball, took a few practice swings, and then glanced down the middle of the fairway. To my surprise, I noticed a huge oak tree off to the right side. I approached my ball, set myself, and swung like you wouldn't believe. The ball bounced off my club like it was made of rubber. It eventually came to stop approximately 150 yards from us in the middle of the fairway. Proud of my hit, I pumped my fist and walked towards my dad. He smiled and gave me a wink.

Little did I know, my first tee off was a sign of good things to come that day.

We ended the round around 2 that afternoon. I was hungry and tired, but energized. After I signed my scorecard, which made my round official, my dad and I walked over to the clubhouse for a mid-afternoon lunch. Numerous people walked by and congratulated me on my round, which surprised me a bit, but it was nice to hear just the same.

"You want to stay and watch a few of the girls finish their rounds?" my dad asked as we ate our lunch.

"Sure."

Eventually my dad and I went back to our hotel room. I was sweaty and tired after all.

At one point I looked at my dad.

"I wonder where I placed today."

"I'm not sure, but I have a feeling you're near the top."

I looked at him in shock.

"Really? Why's that?"

His eyes continued to focus on the TV.

"Because you had a good round, Cali."

Soon, my placement became a distant memory because I

stunk and was hungry. So I took a shower and went to dinner with my dad. We mixed it up and went for Mexican.

The rest of the evening quickly flew by. The television was on in the background, which served as a great distraction for me while I laid in bed. I looked across the room towards my dad. He was fiddling with the computer. I was somewhat perplexed.

He looked at me and smiled.

"Well, it looks like you're in the top 8. We're actually teeing off around noon tomorrow."

I didn't really show much excitement, because I didn't know what to think.

"Did you hear me, Cali? You're in the top 8. That's awesome!"

After the news sunk in, I smiled proudly.

"What time do we need to get there?"

He looked at me as if I asked him how to split an atom.

"Good question. I guess I hadn't thought that far ahead. It says we are teeing off at 11:50. If that's the case, how long do you think you'll need to get ready?"

I blurted out, "9:30."

"Sounds good. We'll get out there around 9:30 tomorrow morning."

Eventually we fell asleep. I fell asleep before my dad did. I must have been tired, because I slept like a log. The morning came rather quickly, so it seemed. I rolled over and noticed it was 7. My dad was up and moving around. Much to my displeasure, he wasn't the quietest in the morning.

"Did you sleep well, Cali?"

Barely awake, I grunted as I stretched.

"Take your time. We're in no hurry."

The next few hours flew by. I got out of bed, showered, put on the cutest blue polo shirt and khakis. Getting dressed was followed by a slow walk down to the lobby with my dad for breakfast. I nibbled on a bagel and sipped on a glass of cranberry juice. I'm not sure who was more excited and anxious -- my dad or me . He wasn't one of those overbearing parents. Instead, he just wanted to see me succeed and enjoy what I was doing.

After we checked out of the hotel, dad drove us to the golf course. Once we arrived, I immediately got to "work" at the driving range and the putting green. The time sure flew by.

In the distance I could hear the crowd "ooh' and "ahh" or applaud enthusiastically.

Eventually it was my time. With me in the lead, dad and I walked towards the first tee and awaited the start of my final round. I was paired with a girl who must have stood some 4 inches taller than me. I was slightly intimidated by her. It didn't help that she was one year older than me, which meant she was a freshman in high school.

"Hey, my name is Cali." I said nervously.

"My name is Cindy." She reached out and shook my hand.

Damn, she even had a tight grip!

We were pretty competitive the first few holes. She was fun to play against, that's for sure. At times we even complimented each other. Much to my disappointment, I couldn't seem to better her score, which made it tough to catch the girls who were in the lead.

As I approached the 17th tee, I glanced at Cindy.

"Well, it's been fun."

"Yes, it has. It stinks we haven't been able to catch the leaders though."

"I haven't," I said with a smile, "but you're pretty darn close," I replied motioning with my head towards the scoreboard.

"Yeah, but I'm running out of time," she replied as she approached the tee box for her 2nd to last tee off of the round.

Both of us teed off without any glitches and were able to make par, which stunk for the both of us, because it meant we were unable to gain any ground. The 18th hole ended much the same way the 17th did. After shaking hands with Cindy and signing my card, my dad and I sat up in the dining area and relaxed while we watched the final few girls finish.

As the leaders completed the last two holes, we noticed something surprising. The leaders were losing ground!

"Um... Dad," I muttered.

"I know," he replied.

My dad began to laugh.

Minutes later, I watched in disbelief as one of the girls hit the ball into the water. I tapped my dad on the wrist.

"Did you see that dad?!"

"I sure did!" He replied.

I tapped my dad on the arm again. I looked around the room and noticed Cindy. She looked at me at the same time and smiled while holding up her crossed fingers.

"No way are the last two going to choke!"

The first one tapped her ball in on par as I watched in agony. The second girl did the same.

"Dang," I muttered.

Even though I didn't win, I did finish in the top ten. Cindy, on the other hand, finished tied for second, which was exciting for her I imagine.

Soon after the awards, my dad loaded my clubs into the pickup and we headed home. Though I was slightly disappointed, I was proud of the way I played. Little did I know, weekends like this toughened me up.

14

Late Spring 8th Grade

A few weeks had passed since the tournament and, though I didn't win, I wasn't disheartened. I was determined to win one at some point. I had hoped Carley would join me at the tournament, but she wasn't able to get away, so she said.

The end of my 8th grade year had finally arrived, which meant more golfing and no school. It didn't take long for my dad, Coach Wilson, and I to hit the links. I think my dad and Coach were ready for school to be out as much as us students. I know Coach Wilson had a long school year. The baseball team fell short and didn't make it to the state tournament. Fortunately, Julio and Jeremy became more accepted. I know it took its toll on Coach though.

As for Carley, she started to notice the boys. Maybe I had other things on my mind, but I was oblivious to them at the time. I certainly wasn't shy. Carley also had a knack for chasing after the bad boys.

Franklin didn't have a deep well of guys to choose from either, but I'm sure the guys felt the same way about us girls. Although I was fresh out of 8th grade, I was already eager to leave the town of Franklin. The town was too cliquish and close minded for me. The way Coach Wilson described the views of some people towards Julio and Jeremy only reinforced my beliefs. I just didn't understand why someone wouldn't be welcomed because of the color of their skin.

One hot summer afternoon, I went over to Brandy's house. She was my older cousin by one year. We were never really very close in our younger years, but as we got older she and I became better friends. She was always boy crazy, which amused me. At times I wondered why I wasn't boy crazy like her. Like me, she also loved sports, even though she didn't play them. Her freshman year she actually made it to nearly every baseball game.

"Hey Brandy!"

I yelled enthusiastically while flashing her the peace sign as I rounded the corner of her house.

In return, my beautiful cousin gave me the biggest grin. She had such a beautiful smile. It was one of those that could lighten the mood if you were depressed.

"Hey Cali!"

I sat down across from her on the big outdoor couch.

"So, are you ready for high school?"

"God, yes," I said without hesitation. "Do you like the teachers?" I asked curiously.

She paused for a moment then a smile raced across her face.

"Yeah, many of them are awesome! You will like them. The worst part of it all is the drama."

"Oh yeah, how so?"

"Oh man, some of the girls can be such bitches. And the boys, well they don't help matters."

It was funny to watch her talk, because she liked to use her hands. She was quite animated.

"What kind of drama?"

Brandy was a little more reserved and tactful than me.

"Oh, just drama with boys. That's all. For example, there were two new boys this year who happened to be black. Man, some of the girls were so up in arms about one of the girls dating the oldest. Just stupid crap like that."

Immediately I knew who she was talking about.

"What are you laughing about?" she asked curiously.

"Oh, nothing," I replied. "I know who you're talking about."

"How so?"

"I golf with Coach Wilson sometimes and my mom and dad hang out with him."

I threw in the golf because I wanted to change the subject.

"That's right. How's that going? Have you been to any tournaments lately?"

"It's going. In a few weeks I'll be going to another tournament, which I'm excited about. Otherwise, I'm just trucking along and trying to improve."

In the back of my mind, I was thankful she had changed

the subject.

"That's so awesome. I'm cousins with a golfer."

Maybe she saw something in me I didn't, but she made me smile. Though she had never seen me golf, she was well aware of my talents.

"Well, I need to head back home. I just wanted to stop by and say hello."

She stood up, whisked her hair to her side, and leaned in for a hug.

"Don't be a stranger. Come by anytime."

Yeah, it was nice catching up with her. Thankfully, in the coming weeks, I was going to be spending more time with her.

15

Fall Freshmen Year

The summer came and went. Outside of my weekly outings on the golf course, summer was pretty quiet. Like most summers, it was unbearably hot and humid. Tragically, one of our own died one late night. I guess the girl, a senior named Nicole, hit a deer while she was on her way home from the lake near Carbondale. I didn't know her, but Brandy did and she was pretty torn up about it. In a small town like Franklin, anytime a teenager dies the community feels the pain. Amazingly, her friend Alexa survived the accident.

The first few months of school were definitely somber, but that didn't stop me from making friends and enjoying my classes. Carley was still in the 8th grade, but that didn't keep us from hanging out or golfing together. I giggled to myself when she complained about her teachers. Yep, I remember those teachers.

Brandy would often pass me in the halls and wave. I was thankful for her friendship. Oftentimes she could be seen with her boyfriend, Kyle, who was one of the Franklin baseball players.

Carley and I participated in several golf tournaments that fall. I even almost won my first tournament, but fell a few strokes short. It was cool to see Cindy again. She finished a few strokes behind me, while Carley didn't place at all. It was quite possibly her worst outing since I had known her. If you play this game long enough, you soon learn everyone has a bad day. Everything that could go wrong sure went wrong for her. I didn't see it, but I guess she hit three balls in a pond on the same hole. Talk about rough!

One afternoon, I was out on my back porch actually completing some homework. The cool breeze was perfect. To my surprise, Carley came around the corner. She definitely didn't seem herself. Instead of the bubbly and goofy girl she normally was, she seemed a little blah.

"Hey, Carley. are you okay?"

She walked over and plopped down on one of the chairs next to me. She remained quiet for a few minutes. I could tell she had been crying, because tears were running down her cheeks, her eyes were red, and she was sniffing.

"You need a tissue?"

She didn't answer.

I waited for about a minute. She still didn't reply to any of my questions.

She finally looked up at me with tears in her eyes.

"My mom and dad are getting a divorce."

Whoa, I didn't see that coming! I awkwardly sat in silence. I didn't know what to say or do. It's not like us teenagers have a manual for situations like that.

"Yeah, my prick of a dad cheated on my mom," she muttered.

"Oh man, I'm so sorry."

I didn't know what to say besides that. I rubbed her leg and hoped I was coming across as supportive.

"Yeah, my mom kicked him out of the house yesterday. I can't believe he did that!"

She paused for a moment.

"So much for golfing."

"What?! No! You can't stop golfing because of this!" I said emphatically.

"Yes I can and I'm going to," she reiterated.

I was at a loss for words. I didn't want to argue with her, but I didn't want her to stop golfing. She had so much potential, plus I enjoyed golfing with her.

"Well, I don't want you to stop, but you're going to do what you're going to do."

"Yeah, no crap," she muttered.

Taken aback, I stood up. I was never much of a pushover.

"Look, I'm sorry about your parents' divorce, but you came over here. Why did you come over here if you were going to be a bitch to me. I'm trying to be supportive. Nah, you can leave now."

Carley looked up at me in silence.

"No, seriously. You can leave. I tried to be supportive and

you shoot me down. I don't need that crap."

Tears were still in her eyes, but I didn't care. Don't get me wrong, I felt so sorry for her, but I wasn't going to let her take her anger out on me. She slowly stood up and somberly walked back the way she came. Looking back I probably could've handled it better.

She stopped and looked at me. Her eyes were red and her face had black lines running down it from the mascara.

"I'm..I'm sorry."

"Yeah, well I'm sorry too."

She looked at me for a few seconds and then, with her head down, she turned and walked away.

16

Fall Freshmen Year

It had been several weeks since Carley had broken the news to me about her parents. Since then, we had hung out a few times, but it was always awkward. The happy girl she once was disappeared. I made attempts to bring her up, but after a while I just gave up.

On the other hand, Brandy was the complete opposite. I'll never forget when she started dating Kyle. Even though I never had an interest in any of the ball players, there were some pretty good looking guys on the team.

I was walking to my second period class when I saw Brandy and Kyle hand in hand. She noticed me and smiled.

"Hey, Cali!" she yelled enthusiastically.

Always a bit more low key, I waved and smiled back.

I looked at Kyle. He was not the most talkative guy around.

"How are you doing, bro?" I asked playfully.

He laughed. There weren't many girls at Franklin who could keep up with me.

"So, are we still on tonight?" Brandy asked me curiously.

"I don't know. Would I be moving in on your territory?" I replied jokingly

"Ah, shut up."

Kyle just stood there.

I'm glad the day flew by. It was probably due to it being Friday.

The final bell rang, which meant the weekend had arrived. The weather was quite pleasant, so I turned down a ride and walked home. Hey, I liked the exercise.

I hung out at my house until it was time to walk over to Brandy's humble abode, which was only a few blocks away.

As I walked up Brandy's driveway, the sun crept down below the horizon, thus illuminating the lights in Brandy's backyard. I walked around the corner of her house. Brandy and Kyle didn't hear me so I yelled " HEY!" really loud.

I fell to my knees in laughter when Brandy dropped her pizza on the ground from being startled.

"You bitch!" She yelled.

I stood up and walked towards her, still laughing. I didn't mean to startle the poor girl, but it was still funny. I threw my arms around her and kissed her on the cheek and then reached to hug Kyle. Even though he was quiet, he was still a pretty good guy. He made her happy.

Though there was a slight breeze, we roughed it. Brandy had an outdoor space heater, which warmed the area up. I felt like I was all grown up as I ate my pizza and drank my soda.

For the next hour, we sat outside and ate as we talked about school, gossiped, and complained about our idiot teachers. At one point, I looked at Kyle.

"So, how's the team looking this year?"

"We should be pretty good. Most of our team is going to be back."

"How good are Julio and Jeremy?"

I was curious what he thought about the two players.

Kyle smiled. "They are both pretty good players. Some of the guys were pretty rough on them last year." He paused. "I don't talk to Julio very often, but Jeremy is pretty cool."

He took a breath.

"So, how's golf?"

"Well, it's chugging along. I'm taking some time off. My dad and I are actually talking about taking a trip to Florida."

I could tell he was jealous. Brandy, on the other hand, seemed oblivious, but then again, this was not news to her.

"Wasn't there a girl you golfed with quite a bit?" he asked curiously.

"Yeah, Carley, but I haven't talked to her for a while."

Brandy sat up.

"Why? What happened?"

"Oh, her dad cheated on her mom, so I guess to get back at him she stopped golfing."

Brandy and Kyle looked at each other perplexed.

"I know right," I added humorously. "She was a pretty good golfer as well. But whatever."

Brandy smiled. "But not as good as you, cuz."

Not wanting to appear overly cocky, I tried to play it down and act surprised.

The night soon came to a close. It was hard to believe Thanksgiving was only a few weeks away and that Christmas would soon follow.

17

Late Fall Freshmen Year

I loved the holidays because I got to sleep in. I also loved the food. Thank goodness I worked out because my mom was an awesome cook! In many ways I didn't truly understand or appreciate the work she put into fixing us dinner until I was older and had to fix my own meals.

It had been awhile since I talked to Carley and, well, I missed her. Our argument always bothered me. From time to time, my dad would ask me if I had talked to her. I would ask why, but he would never give me a definitive answer.

I was in my room contemplating the week ahead of me. Christmas was right around the corner after all. My parents were downstairs and the TV was blaring. I think they were watching the local news. Not that it really matters. The TV volume humored me.

I fumbled through my phone until I came upon Carley's number. The other end of the phone rang and rang, which was not like Carley. She was always quick to answer the phone. When it came time to leave a message, I hung up. I was disappointed she didn't answer.

After I hung up my phone, I quietly relaxed on my bed. After several minutes, I determined it was time to go down and let my parents know I was still alive. They hadn't seen me for a few hours and I had a tendency to be extremely quiet while in my room.

Once downstairs, I sat in my favorite plush chair next to my dad.

"What have you been up to? You were quiet up there."

I wasn't feeling the most upbeat and he probably could tell. He was good like that.

"Yeah, I was just relaxing. I tried calling Carley, but she didn't answer." I paused. "Do you see her much at school? She hasn't been the same since her parents filed for their divorce. She seems much angrier." I added.

I sat next to my dad and pondered things. I didn't understand why she was so angry at the world. Hell, I was angry at her. She had so much golfing potential it killed me.

Eventually, I went to bed with Carley on my mind. The next day I woke up refreshed. It was the weekend, there was a slight chill in the air, and Christmas was around the corner. I wasn't going to wait around for her to call me.

After downing a hearty breakfast consisting of cereal, juice, and bacon, I ran upstairs determined to talk to Carley. I wanted to know how she was doing. I ran into my room, closed my door, and jumped onto my bed like a ten year old.

The other end of the phone rang several times.

To my surprise I heard a sleepy "hello" on the other end.

"Hey, Carley! How are you doing?"

"Oh. Hey, Cali."

I don't think she was fully awake.

She continued. "What's up?"

"I have missed you, so I just wanted to call and say hello." I added.

"Ah well, that's nice of you," she added.

"I'd love to hang out with you sometime," I replied.

There was a pause on the other end.

"Sorry, Cali. I will be busy the next few weeks."

My excitement turned to utter disappointment.

"Oh, okay," I muttered.

"Yeah, well, sorry. Well I have to run, Cali. Buh Bye."

She hung up before I even had a chance to say goodbye. Saddened, I looked at the wall for several minutes. Several tears ran down my face.

I laid quietly in my room for several minutes. The whole time I wiped away my tears. I looked down at my phone. My radio was on in the background and it happened to be playing one of those folksy uplifting songs.

Well, I'm no longer reaching out to her

I wrote Brandy in a text.

About a minute later my phone buzzed. It was a text from Brandy. She was always quick to respond.

Well she's a bitch. It's her loss. You don't need her.

Appreciative of Brandy's support, I quickly responded,

Thanks!

with a cute smiley face attached in the text.

18

Winter Freshmen Year

Another Christmas came and went. My parents got me a killer new driver for golf and the cutest outfit for my next tournament. Christmas evening we went over to the Wilson's, which was fun as always. I always wondered why they didn't have children, because they were so good around them. Of course, out of respect, I never asked.

Christmas vacation came to an end. I sauntered into my first period class. By no means was I ready to start back to school, but I had no choice. Quietly, I walked to the first desk I saw nearest to the door and sat down.

Franklin High School was small, so it was always obvious when a new student appeared. A new girl walked into class and sat down in an open seat near the front. She looked lost. Her long, straight, blonde hair and blue eyes immediately caught my attention. She was beautiful, I immediately thought.

My first class zipped by. Thank goodness, because I don't think I could've taken anymore math if my life depended on it. Solving for X was just not one of my joys in life. The bell rang, releasing us from our first period class. We all immediately stood up and moved towards the door like a band of prisoners attempting to break out of jail.

I weaved through the halls like a race car driver at the

Daytona 500. I passed Brandy who, of course, was holding hands with Kyle. After I stopped for a sip of water at the water fountain, I walked into my English class. Though I had no qualms with reading, I wasn't a fan of the books my teachers seemed to pick. They were boring!

To my surprise, the new girl walked into the room grasping her schedule. She looked around the room perplexed until she was able to locate the teacher. After confirming she was in the right class, she glanced around the room. I hoped she would find her way towards me, since there were no assigned seats. The only ones assigned to seats were a couple of overly excited boys that never learned what it meant to shut up. They, of course, were placed in the various corners of the room.

I flashed her a smile. She shyly smiled back and sat down in the seat directly in front of me.

"Hey, my name is Cali."

Unfortunately, not everyone at Franklin High School would have even said that much.

"My name is Megan."

"Where are you from, Megan?"

"I'm from Marion."

I couldn't get over how beautiful her smile was. It was captivating. She had one of those smiles the boys were going to fall for.

"I take it you're from here?"

"Yep," I said while rolling my eyes. "Born and raised. Don't let the people here intimidate you."

She laughed.

"I won't. This is not my first rodeo. I'm actually from the St. Louis area."

The bell rang, causing students to quickly run to desks.

"Well, I guess I better turn around. I don't want to get into trouble the first day."

Her sarcasm humored me.

At Franklin High School the average class size was around 20 students, which wasn't bad. Megan was in most of my classes which I was excited about. Every time she appeared in the same class as mine, I teased her by saying "you again" or "I see you're following me."

Thankfully she had a good sense of humor. I didn't know her, but I had good vibes about her. It's not like Franklin was the easiest town to move to.

After the final bell rang to end the school day, I walked through the halls towards the main doors. As I neared the main doors, I was slowed by one of the other Freshmen girls. For some reason slow walkers especially aggravated me. Of course it had to be Jamie. Jamie was one of those students that just rubbed me the wrong way. It's not like she ever did anything wrong. She wasn't a bad kid. I did think she was lazy when it came to school, but otherwise she was just one of those students that just aggravated me no matter what she did. She could've landed on the moon and I would've found something wrong with her.

"Can you move your slow ass?" I muttered.

Jamie turned and gave me a pissy look, which I honestly don't blame her for doing.

"Well, move your ass around me bitch," she responded sternly.

I was in no mood for a confrontation even though I started it. I moaned, rolled my eyes, and walked around her.

I quickly passed her through the main doors of the school. As I walked towards Brandy and Kyle, I couldn't get Megan out of my mind.

"Well look at you," Brandy hollered when she saw me.

She tapped Kyle on the shoulder.

"Well, look who's cheesin."

I didn't know I was smiling that much, but I was in a pretty good mood.

"Shut up, Brandy."

I tried to be serious, but I couldn't wipe my stupid smile off my face.

She followed me with her eyes rather suspectedly as I got into the car.

"What?!" asked, throwing my hands in the air.

"Oh nothing," she said with a smile.

After they took me home, I went down to the basement and lifted some weights and ran on the treadmill. It wasn't a workout room until I started golfing. I guess my dad saw the need to create a place for me to lift, so I could get stronger. At first he had to nag me, but after a while it became a habit. The more I lifted, the farther I noticed my ball began to fly.

Even though I wasn't excited about starting a new semester, my tune quickly changed.

19

Winter Freshmen Year

The first week back from Christmas break breezed by. Each morning I was excited to see Megan walk into class. I knew the guys at Franklin High didn't do it for me. Don't get me wrong I was attracted to guys, I just had no inclination to date any of them. Most of the guys came across as good ole country boys, which I was NOT attracted to. Many of them were very closed minded as well. There were a few girls that I had noticed and were actually physically attracted to at my school, but I didn't think much about it at the time. I was always curious what it was like to kiss or even date a girl, but I always kept it to myself. Partly out of embarrassment and partly out of fear. I was afraid of what my friends and family would think. Heck, I had never even kissed a boy, so I was super confused.

Living in a small conservative town like Franklin didn't help things much either. I was never much of one to fit in, at least in Franklin. I definitely didn't want to be shunned by my peers either.

When Megan walked into my Algebra class the Monday after the break, solving for X became a lot more interesting. I was so excited and scared all at the same time. Yep, I definitely had a thing for her, but what exactly did that mean? I also knew I wanted to kiss her, but what did that really mean? It was all very confusing and frustrating. Was this normal? Was I the only one that felt this way or were there others like me?

Opening up to someone about your feelings is more than scary. Living in Franklin didn't help matters much either. Thankfully, not only was Brandy my cousin, she was also my friend.

I walked over to Brandy's house. Kyle was at a basketball game and she had no desire to go, so she invited me over for pizza.

While we ate our pizza up in her room, Brandy and I talked about the normal things -- boys, which I had no interest in talking about at that moment, school, and the upcoming spring. I grabbed the last slice and commenced biting into it. Pepperoni was always my favorite, but this one had ham and pineapple. Brandy was never one much for pepperoni apparently.

Brandy set down her glass of soda.

"So, tell me. Who is it?"

Caught off guard, I nearly choked on my pizza.

"Who is what?"

I knew damn well what she was asking.

"Come on, Cali. You haven't been this goofy for a long time. It must be some boy, but hey, I could be wrong."

Yeah, she was wrong, but not totally off base. I set down

my pizza and wiped my mouth. I looked away for a moment. Admitting I was attracted to a girl was scary enough, but telling my cousin was equally scary. I didn't know what she would say or do. Of all the students at Franklin High School, I probably respected Brandy the most, but it was still scary. She was my cousin, but she was also my friend.

"Um, well um, you're right, Brandy. I do like someone and I have to admit I'm at a loss."

I was so nervous my palms were sweating.

"At a loss? Why?" She threw her hands in the air. "What's his name? Who is it?"

I looked away and then back at her.

"Well… it's a she."

"Wait, what?!"

She looked shocked, which of course made me even more nervous.

"Well, okay. What's her name?"

I smiled nervously, because I was worried she would judge me.

"It's Megan, the new girl."

"Does she know?"

"Noooo." I paused momentarily. "Shit, I don't even know if she likes girls. I have this feeling she does. She's been passing that vibe you know?"

Brandy nodded her head.

"I didn't know you were interested in girls."

"Honestly, I didn't either. I mean I knew, but I didn't. I have never had a desire to date any of the guys from here in town. I just figured it was because they're so damn immature and closed minded." I paused. "Yeah, I've noticed girls on T.V., at school...you know, but I just never thought about dating a girl."

"Yeah, guys can sure be immature." Brandy added with a laugh.

"I just always thought a girl had to be a butch to like other girls."

"Huh." Her eyes looked towards the ceiling and then back towards me. "I guess I never thought about it until now."

She paused again.

"Hmmmmm."

"Hmm, what?" I asked.

"I wonder if there is anyone else at school that is gay or bisexual?"

Neither of us had the answer to her question so we sat on her bed in silence.

"Well, can you please keep this between us?" I asked.

"You know me, girl. Mum's the word."

She motioned with her finger to her mouth.

I grabbed one of the pillows from the bed and held it tightly and yelled out an expletive. Defeated, I looked at

Brandy.

"Brandy, I'm scared."

A tear ran down my cheek. Emotions I had kept bottled up began to come up from the depths of my body.

Brandy rolled her lower lip. She clearly felt bad for me.

"Come here, sweetie," she said with her arms open.

I scooted in and leaned up against her. My hair partly covered my face.

"Why does everything have to be so confusing, Brandy?"

She kissed me softly on my head, but she didn't say anything. She didn't need to.

After several minutes, I sat up. My cheeks were black because my mascara had run down my cheeks.

"I bet I'm a hot mess, aren't I?"

Brandy smiled as she took her right index finger and wiped some of the mascara from my face. "No more than me most of the time," she added.

I pounded my fists onto the bed several times and yelled. "Shit!" I continued. "I hate this." Then I took the pillow I was holding and threw it across the room.

I took two deep breaths.

I looked at Brandy. "For starters, I'm afraid I come out and put my emotions on my sleeve and she rejects me. I'm also afraid of what everyone else will say."

Brandy laughed. "C'mon girl, when have you ever given a

fuck what anyone else has thought. That's what I love about you. You're your own person. I'm soooo jealous of you."

"Really?" That shocked me.

"Yeah... really," she emphasized.

"Ha… why?"

"C'mon Cali, you're always so confident. You have a take no prisoners attitude. I wish I could be like you."

I looked at her, looked away, and then back at her. I couldn't help but smile. I guess I needed to hear her vote of confidence.

Brandy reached for my hand.

"I couldn't even imagine what you are dealing with inside. All I can say is that I'm here for you. Okay?"

She gently grabbed my chin and turned my head towards hers because I was looking straight ahead. "You understand me Cali. I'm serious. I'm here for you like I know you'd be for me."

I began to cry again. Brandy wrapped her arms around me and rocked me. She was so sweet and caring. Gently, she kissed me on the head.

"It's going to be okay. I promise." she whispered.

After several minutes I sat up and wiped my face. It was covered in makeup after all.

"Do your parents know you're interested in girls?"

"Oh, hell no …I don't think they would be all judgy… God,

I hope not."

"Well, just be yourself."

The conversation eventually drifted from me, thankfully, to Brandy and her dating exploits with Kyle and our classes. I never told her but I was actually jealous of her. She had such a good thing going even if she wished should be like me!

20

Winter Freshmen Year

Monday arrived after a not so exciting weekend. I sat at the same desk, but this time I hoped Megan would sit next to me. My heart skipped a beat when she DID. I was so excited, though I worked hard to hide it. Hell, I didn't even know if she liked girls or not, though I had that feeling she did. I didn't really know how I felt. I just knew I was attracted to her.

For the next week and a half, I did my best to play it cool. I complimented her when I felt it was warranted and created small talk whenever I could. She did the same in return. Except for Brandy, no one else knew how I felt. I was afraid of what everyone would say. Finally, after a week and a half I decided to take a leap. It was a cold, rainy, Wednesday morning.

During English class, she was in the seat next to me. She looked at me and smiled.

"Hey Cali, how are you? You look cute today. That sweater looks good on you."

I nervously smiled back. Geeze, I loved her smile AND she thought I looked cute!

"It's cold out there this morning, isn't it?"

In the background I could hear the radiator rumble away. That thing must have been 100 year old.

She took a sip of her coffee.

"You want to hang out later this week?" I asked.

"Sure, I'd love to." She replied as she continued to smile while she played with her hair.

"Alright, awesome." I replied.

The bell rang for class to start.

Later that evening I began to get cold feet, so who better to call than Brandy. Thankfully she was home.

"Hey, what's up gorgeous?" she said playfully upon answering the phone.

"Oh nothing," I muttered.

Brandy was always an amazingly upbeat girl.

There was a pause.

"Shut up. What's bothering ya?"

She knew I had called for a reason.

"I'm nervous about Friday."

There was another awkward pause.

"Oh, I never did tell yah. Megan and I are getting together Friday night."

"That's awesome, Cali. Are you excited?"

"Well, that's the reason I'm calling you actually. What if I mess this up? Oh shit Brandy, I'm having a breakdown."

Brandy began to giggle.

"What's so funny?"

"Nothing! I've never heard you freak out over someone before. It's kinda funny."

Frazzled, I laid on my bed and kicked my feet up and down.

"This sucks!" I yelled.

"Nah, think of it as a journey. Just get together and have a good time. You never really know if someone is interested in you until you try. It's a bitch girl, but don't let that stop you. Be yourself! You're an awesome person."

There was a pause.

"I was nervous the first time I got together with Kyle. Again, just be yourself."

"Thanks, Brandy."

I felt a little better, but I was still quite nervous. So much so I felt a little queasy. I guess in the end, I had to be myself and just see where things went. I hung up the phone and stared quietly at the wall. My hair laid in front of my face all disheveled from my earlier little tantrum.

Finally, I turned off the bedroom lights. Though it was still early in the evening and I had homework to complete, I was ready for some sleep.

Thursday and Friday quickly slipped by, thank God! Megan sat in front of me and talked about her classes. Geeze, I loved her smile and her hair! Oh her hair! It was long and wavy. The whole time I wondered --

Did she like me?

Was she hanging out with me to be friends or more?

Was I a lesbian?

Was I bisexual?

Does she think I'm cute?

What would it be like to run my hands through her hair?

Ugh! Questions ran through my head and that drove me absolutely nuts! I didn't know anyone else in town that was gay, lesbian, or bisexual. In the past, the few students that did come out as gay or lesbian were shunned almost immediately, which didn't help my cause.

Thankfully, my parents didn't ask me a whole lot of questions prior to Megan coming over. Hell, if they had, I would've just brushed it off as her being a new girl in school and they wouldn't have known the difference. At least, that's what I told myself.

I stood up in my room looking through my closet. I couldn't decide what to wear! Shit! Finally, I grabbed a pink top that was hanging in my closet. I stood in front of the mirror and asked myself what would look good with the top I held in my hand. After several seconds of deep contemplation, I dashed across my room and found the cutest pair of jeans.

I looked at the clock. I had twenty minutes before Megan was to arrive. I guess her parents were bringing her over. I looked at my hands and noticed I was shaking. Was I nervous? Was I scared? "Yes" and "Yes"!

Get it together. I mumbled.

Finally, the doorbell rang! It was her.

I stood in front of the mirror and did everything I could to calm myself down. I even counted to ten.

Muffled, because my door was closed, I heard my dad. "Honey, you have company."

I looked at the mirror, took a deep breath, and then smiled. I turned to go down stairs when Megan walked through the door. Damn, she looked amazing in her jeans and sweatshirt. I was immediately nervous again.

"Hey Megan, how are you?" I said shyly.

She smiled.

21

Late Winter Freshmen Year

The next few weeks went by rather nicely for Megan and I. She sat in front of me every day in most of our classes and I loved it. Why did I love it? Well I loved talking to her and I was more than attracted to her but I still wasn't sure if she was into me or not. Sometimes we even walked to our next class together but in the back of my mind I was worried what other people thought. It was really nerve racking. Is this how it's supposed to be? I wondered multiple times a day.

One evening we were studying for a test in my room, at least that's what I told my parents. To my surprise she put her books down and looked at me.

"So? Are you ever going to kiss me?"

In shock I sat up and looked at her. I didn't quite know what to say or think. I immediately grew nervous even though I was super excited. I wanted to kiss her, but I had never kissed anyone before. What if I wasn't good enough? What if I didn't do it right? What if she was unimpressed? Shit, was this how it was always going to be?

Finally, I leaned over and put my shaking right palm up to her face. At this point I had decided it was do or die. There was no going back.

I paused as I looked at her eyes. She smiled which made

me smile. Her lips were cherry red which I loved.

Slowly, I slid my right palm off her face towards the back of her head. Once my hand reached her hair, I slowly ran my hand through it. Her hair was soft and flowing. I loved it.

I hesitated, and then her lips met mine. It was amazing though scary at the same time. I hadn't had any experience in the kissing category. The only kissing action I had seen was in the movies.

After a few seconds we both opened our eyes and smiled at each other.

There was a silence.

She giggled innocently. She put her left hand up to my hand and lightly caressed my hand with her face. "That was nice."

She leaned in and nestled herself into me.

For once in my life, I felt important to someone besides my parents and I loved it.

As tough as it was, we re-focused our efforts on our studies. The evening came to a close when her dad pulled into the driveway.

She stood up and smiled. "So I guess I'll see you tomorrow?"

I stood up and smiled back. "I hope so."

There was an awkward pause.

I wanted to ask her what this all meant but I chickened

out. This all was a first for me.

After walking her to the door, I sprinted back upstairs. While passing my parents I stopped to wish them a good night. Like every other evening they were in their normal spot, my dad on the couch and my mom in the recliner, watching the local news.

As soon as I got into my room I closed my door and picked up my phone

My hands shook with nervous excitement as I texted Brandy.

Can you keep a secret?

Sure, why?

Megan and I kissed tonight

There was a pause, and then my phone rang.

I immediately answered. "Hey Brandy!"

"Hey Cali, how are you?"

I had a huge grin on my face. I'm sure if I looked in the mirror all my teeth would have been showing.

"So you two kissed huh? Well that's exciting."

There was another pause.

"Did she kiss you or did you kiss her?"

I looked up towards the ceiling. "Well we were studying and she put her books down, looked at me, and asked me if I was going to kiss her or not."

Brandy giggled. "Wow, look at you, busting the moves." There was a pause "So, what was it like?"

"Pretty scary. I was probably all clunky."

She laughed.

"Yeah, I remember the first time I kissed a boy. It was definitely awkward. Nothing like what you see in the movies, that's for sure."

As much as I wanted to continue our conversation I was getting tired. "Well I don't want to keep you. Thanks for calling."

"You're welcome, Cali. You're such a sweetie."

"Thanks Brandy, I love you."

"I love you too." and with that we both hung up.

22

Late Winter Freshmen Year

The next few days were a little less awkward for me. Whenever my schedule allowed it, I walked with her to her next class. From time to time she sent me little notes of motivation and words of caring via text throughout the day. Of course, I would always gleefully respond.

I was sitting in class one afternoon. I can't remember which class it was, I just know Megan wasn't in the class. I was doodling in my notebook when my phone buzzed. I wanted to pull my phone out of my purse, but I was afraid to get my phone taken up. Some of the teachers didn't want to see our phones on our desk at all. I could understand why, it just meant I had to be sneaky about it.

Much to my satisfaction it was Megan who had texted me.

Hey what are you doing this evening?

I read her text and smiled. Quickly my fingers went to work.

Nothing why?

Come on over if you want

Before I had a chance to reply, she sent me another text.

I need help with math and besides I want to see you xo

I read her text a couple of times. I couldn't help but smile.

Alright, I'll be there...7 good?

Perfect

After getting home, I worked out and showered. My mom was in the kitchen rummaging about and preparing dinner.

"Hey mom, you mind if I go over to Megan's to work on some math around 7?"

She never looked up as she sliced away on a tomato.

"No, not all. You two seem to be hitting it off," she said with a smile.

She didn't know half of it I thought.

My mom stopped slicing her tomato and looked at me. "Well, we'll take you over after dinner and we'll pick you up around 9. How's that sound?"

"That's perfect! Thanks!"

She went back to her preparing our dinner. "Get the

dishes out, will you hun?" She asked before I had a chance to escape.

After having another amazing dinner fixed by my mom, my dad drove me over to Megan's house. We had been working on our math for about an hour. The TV was on in the background, but it was more for noise I think. Both of us were on our stomachs laying across her bed.

I was working on a math problem when I began to feel a hand across my back. I had never had anyone rub my back before. It felt good. Slowly, she moved her hand up my back and through my hair. I put my pencil down and looked at her. I definitely wasn't going to get any work done with her rubbing my back, that's for sure!

We both smiled at each other. Like the first night we kissed, her lips were cherry red.

I smiled. "You know," I said nervously, "I really love how red your lips are."

"Well, why don't you kiss them," she said with a grin.

I paused and then leaned in and kissed her. As much as I didn't want to stop, I pulled away. Her lips not only were cherry red, they had the taste of cherries, which I loved.

"So I'm curious, have you always been attracted to girls?" I asked.

There was silence. "That's why I moved here from Marion."

"Really, how so?"

She took a deep breath. "I think I started realizing when I was in the 6th grade I wasn't attracted to boys but was attracted to girls instead. No, I mean I knew it before the 6th grade, but that's when it really hit me that dating guys wasn't an option."

She paused while she looked around the room.

"Anyways, to make a long story short my parents moved me here because I was getting bullied in Marion… So yeah, that's my story. What about you?"

I took a deep breath. "Yeah, I have always noticed girls but never thought about it until I saw you walk into class."

"You mean that you were attracted to girls sexually?"

I nervously laughed. "Yep."

She smiled. "Well I'm attracted to you too."

"You are?" I asked while blushing.

She smiled. "What's not to like about you? You're athletic, smart, you're a smart ass, and you don't take crap."

I continued to blush. "Thanks, that means a lot."

There was a pause. I bit my upper lip and smiled. "Yeah I remember when you walked into class that first day. I loved your hair, it's so beautiful. I love how you send me little notes throughout the day. It makes me smile."

She smiled. "Good."

We kissed again, but this time it was more of just a peck. The desire to kiss her was overwhelming. I think partly because

I had never kissed anyone before and I loved it.

She looked towards the ceiling. "I know it may sound strange that my parents moved here of all places."

I couldn't help but smile. She smiled in return. Then, much to my delight, she leaned and kissed me on the lips.

"We better get back to work," she said after she kissed me.

I happily sighed. "Do we have to?"

Sadly, my dad texted me moments later. He was on his way over to Megan's house to pick me up. The evening came to an end.

23

Late Winter Freshmen Year

January turned into February. Megan and I continued to hang out during the week and sometimes on the weekends. Valentine's Day had finally arrived. In the past I was never really excited about Valentine's Day but this time was different. I was on my way to class when I noticed Brandy. Of course, Brandy held a big ole' teddy bear in her arms from Kyle. Kyle was all about Brandy, but he definitely wasn't the teddy bear type.

"Hey Cali!" she yelled.

Excited, I waved back. In my arms I held a small, dark, brown, fluffy teddy bear and a card along with a pink plush pillow with a heart on it. I couldn't believe it, Brandy was by herself. Normally Kyle was with her.

"Where's Kyle?"

"Oh, he's down in the gym throwing. Baseball is only a few weeks away and he and a few of the others are down there." She paused for a second. "Where's Megan?" she asked with a devilish grin.

"I don't know." I paused. "It's strange. Sometimes I see her before class while other times she just appears as the bell is ringing."

"Huh, that's strange," replied Brandy. "Well, this is for

you."

She held out a big ole fluffy light brown teddy bear.

I opened my arms excitedly.

"Well, this is for you Brandy."

Brandy smiled when I handed her a card and the plush pillow.

"Thanks Cali!"

The warning bell sounded, which I always got a kick out of. The fact that we needed to be warned the final bell was about to ring always made me smile. Brandy and I hugged each other one more time. As cheesy as it was, we both were excited about the day. I wound through the hall dodging students like a spaceship dodges asteroids.

Slightly depressed because I hadn't seen Megan, I sauntered into my first period class. As soon as I sat down in my seat, she wandered into the room. I immediately noticed her eyes were bloodshot. I innocently concluded that she must have been up all night studying.

She sat in the seat directly in front of me. I looked at her and she awkwardly looked at me. Even though the morning hadn't gone as planned, I was still glad to see her.

"Are you okay? Your eyes are a little bloodshot."

She shrugged off the question. "Yeah I'm fine… Oh, this is for you." she added shoving a card my way as if it was a chore.

I was a little disappointed in the way she was acting, but I also wondered if I was being overly dramatic. Shyly, I handed her the bear I had bought her. Even though I was proud of the gift I got her, I wondered and worried what she thought.

During the class period I pretended to listen to my teacher but, come on, who actually listens to their teacher when you have one hundred other things on your mind! I wanted to open the card she gave me, but something inside of me told me to wait.

With the class half over and the teacher lost in their own world, I decided it was a good time to open Megan's card. I noticed she had written a short note, but I glanced through the card first which made me smile. The card said something about being there and important to her. As soon as I was done reading through the card, I began reading her note she had written to me.

> Dear Cali,
> As glad as I am you came into my life I have to say I'm not the one for you. We are not the ones for each other. Words can't say how thankful I was when

I looked up at her and then back down at the card. That bitch! She had the nerve to give me an I'm dumping you note, but yet she took my card and teddy bear! Oh, I was so pissed. For the next twenty minutes I stared into space until it was time to leave for the next class.

At one point she turned around, but I refused to make eye contact with her. She asked me something, but I ignored her. FINALLY, the bell rang which allowed me to escape.

In between classes I walked by Brandy, pissed at the world, so I didn't even notice her.

"Hey! Are you okay, girlie?"

I looked at her and shrugged my shoulders. No. I wasn't okay, but I was in no mood to talk to her about it. Even if tears were in my eyes.

Always the friend, she stopped me by grabbing my arm.

"Wait, what's wrong, Cali?"

Tears had built up in my eyes. As hard as I tried to hide it, she noticed them.

"That... that..." I stammered. "That bitch! Damn, what was I thinking?!"

A few students walked by and glanced at me. Even though I didn't think I was very loud, apparently I was loud enough to create a minor scene.

"Why? What happened?"

I angrily gave the card to Brandy. She took the card and opened it up and began to read it. From time to time she would look up at me. The tears I worked hard to hide began to stream down my face uncontrollably.

I looked up at the hallway clock.

"Damn, the bell is going to ring," I muttered.

"Everything okay, ladies?" a deep voice asked. I looked over and walking our way was Coach Wilson.

Shit. He was the last one I needed to see, since he was friends with my dad.

"Oh hey, Mr. Wilson, yeah... Cali's having some girl issues. Everything's okay though."

Brandy had a way of talking to the teachers. I never really mastered that ability, especially when I was upset.

Coach Wilson looked at me and then Brandy. "Go into the bathroom. When she's ready, come and get me, and I'll write you both a pass."

"Thanks, sir," I muttered as I softly wiped away my tears.

A few minutes later, after some mild screaming and yelling, I emerged from the bathroom. Even though I was still upset, I felt much better.

Brandy smiled.

"Next time you're going to pace like you did in there, don't wear heels."

We went on our merry way after we acquired our passes from Mr. Wilson. The last person I wanted to see was Megan, who was in my class. I walked in, handed the teacher my pass and sat down near the door. It was a challenge, but I refused to look at Megan. Throughout much of the class period I felt twenty sets of eyes piercing through me. I wanted to disappear into the wall.

The class was in the middle of a quiz, which really sucked because I wasn't in the right mindset. At the time, I had the attention span of a gnat.

After I failed that quiz, the rest of the day dragged on. It was especially torturous because Megan was in many of the same classes as me. When the final bell rang I escaped from the room, walked quickly down the hall, and ran out of the building quicker than I ever have.

As I made my way through the parking lot, I noticed Megan. To my surprise, she was with Jamie and they were walking together towards John's pickup.

No wonder Megan's eyes were bloodshot that morning. She was smoking weed with Jamie and John. I never had any use for Jamie because of her laziness, but John? Oh, I especially disliked him. At Franklin High School he was a known druggie, which was sad because he was quite athletic and very charming -- assuming you could look past his racist tendencies, use of drugs, and overall laziness. Then again, he was not much different from half the student body. Some were just better at hiding those characteristics than others.

The weather was quite pleasant, so I walked home and thought about the day. The days were getting a little longer. As much as I wanted to go to the driving range and whack a few balls, it was still too cold.

Not long after I arrived home, my dad did as well. I was downstairs working out when he walked through the back door. I knew it was him because he clomped around the house, unlike my mom who walked like a dainty mouse.

He opened the door and yelled down to me.

"You down there, hun?"

I cringed when I heard him. I hoped Coach didn't say anything to him.

"Yeah, I'm down here!"

"Okay!"

What? That was it? I delayed my venture upstairs as long as possible. Either nothing was said to my dad or my dad had determined it wasn't worth asking me about. I'm glad he didn't, because I am a terrible liar, especially if pressed.

After dinner, which was a quiet affair, I ventured upstairs and read. While in my room, I felt sorry for myself. It was quite a pathetic scene. Silently, I whimpered in the dark until I fell asleep.

24

Early Spring Freshmen Year

Even though we were cordial in the classroom, I had nothing to do with Megan outside of school nor did I want to. A couple of mornings before school, I noticed she was hanging out with a group of students notorious for their drug use. I definitely didn't want to be a part of that.

I was in class daydreaming about golf when Jamie and Megan walked into class together.

Megan looked at me. She had a subtle smirk on her face and it was directed at me, or at least I felt like it was. They walked to the far end of the class, which was fine as far as I was concerned.

I looked in their direction. I wondered what in the hell they were doing together. I was immediately jealous of Jamie. Not long after they entered the room, the class bell rang. I was glad because that meant I could take my mind off of them. Of course the last thing I wanted to see was them together throughout the day. I mean, Jamie of all people.

Around 5:30 that evening, I walked over to Brandy's house excited to down a few slices of pizza and relax for the evening. Of course I wanted to vent, but just how much would be in question with Kyle around? I was glad to see I arrived before he did. He had baseball practice, so he had to clean up and shower.

I plopped down on the porch couch with a glass of tea in hand. Brandy followed me with her not so healthy soda, but hey, I'm not judging.

"You'll never guess who I saw Megan with today?" I chirped angrily.

Brandy nestled into her chair and smiled. She pretended to think.

"Let me think. It wasn't Jamie, was it? You know that little skank pothead."

My mouth dropped to the floor.

Brandy started to laugh.

"Why? Are you surprised I know this?"

I sat on the couch speechless and a little upset. Brandy never shared this nugget of news with me. She could tell I was upset.

"C'mon Cali, get over her. Megan does drugs. You know that and I know that. She's trouble with a capital T."

She paused for a moment.

"Then there's Jamie. I mean, where do we start with her? I mean, she's a sweetheart and all, but anyone that dates her is someone you don't need to agonize over. It's as simple as that."

As much as I wanted to argue with her, I couldn't. Brandy had some valid points and she knew it.

"Besides, Golf is starting shortly and you don't have time for girl drama," Brandy added.

I grinned. "Thanks Brandy!"

We both took a sip of our drinks.

"Well look who's here!" I yelled out. "Do I need to leave, Kyle?" I asked jokingly.

Shyly, he sat down next to Brandy. He always seemed a little awkward around her, but that was part of his charm. He was definitely not a player.

"So how's the team looking?"

I was always a fan of sports and Julio, their senior pitcher, was someone I admired. Even though the school wasn't very big, I only knew about Julio through Coach Wilson. I always took the stories from other students with a grain of salt since the story tellers weren't always the most reliable.

"Yeah, the team is looking pretty good. I'll be pitching a little more this year, but Julio will be the main guy."

"When's your first game?"

"Our first game is next week," he added.

Brandy sat there nodding her head as if she knew, but I knew she didn't.

After we ate our pizza and talked about the goings-ons at Franklin High School, I decided it was time to head home before it got too late. Especially since I had a golf outing with my dad the next morning.

I walked through the back door next to the kitchen and into the living room. My mom and dad were in their respective spots watching the news on the TV. At the time I thought they were so boring, but as I got older, I grew to appreciate those quiet evenings.

My dad looked up at me and smiled.

"How are Brandy and Kyle, hun?"

"Oh, they're fine."

I plopped down on the couch to talk since I hadn't seen them all day.

My mom looked at me and smiled.

"Have you talked to Megan lately?"

I was kind of surprised my mom asked me about her, but then again, my parents always had a way of catching me off guard.

"Nope, I haven't talked to her and quite honestly it's for the best. I have a feeling she's doing drugs."

My Mom shook her head.

"That's too bad. Well, you are making the right decision then."

I wanted to change the subject, but with my parents, I had to just let the issue die. Exclaiming I had no desire to talk about it would never work and just create more questions. If not then, another time.

Thankfully my dad did change the subject.

"So are you ready for tomorrow?"

"Oh yeah and I'm going to beat you!" I exclaimed.

"Well, we'll see."

Like me, he had a grin on his face.

"I'm going to make a bold prediction, dad."

"Oh, what's that Cali?"

I playfully pointed my finger at him and smiled even though I pretended to be all serious.

"I'm going to beat you several times this summer, mark my word."

My mom grabbed her empty glass. The remaining ice cubes clanked in her glass as little droplets fell from the glass. She stood up and smiled.

"You two are too much. I'm heading to the kitchen. Do you guys need anything?"

"Nope, I'm fine Mom. Thanks," I chimed. "I'm heading upstairs anyways."

I unraveled myself from the seat I was in, stretched, and went upstairs. Though it wasn't really that late, I wanted to get plenty of rest for my match in the morning with my dad.

The next morning I rolled over when my alarm loudly buzzed. I slowly sat up, yawned, and glanced towards my window. It was still dark out, but I could tell the sun was climbing over the horizon like a hiker on a steep hill. The sun created this cool orangish glow which appeared through my window. The birds happily chirped in the trees which partially blocked the glow of the sun. I couldn't help but smile.

I jumped out of my bed after a few agonizing minutes of motivational thought and sauntered towards the shower. After a quick shower, I got dressed, and then clomped down the stairs. Of course, my dad was already up and awaiting my presence.

My dad could tell I wasn't fully awake when I appeared. He was standing next to the kitchen counter and sipping some coffee while browsing through the local newspaper.

"Still asleep, are yah?" he asked.

I just grunted as I put some butter on my toast.

My dad smiled.

After I finished my juice and toast, I quietly walked over and put my dishes in the sink.

My dad looked at his watch.

"Shall we go?"

I looked at him and grinned. I was ready to hit the links. I just needed a ride there and a partner to golf with. My dad just happened to be that person.

We quietly piled into my dad's pickup. The big orange ball, called the sun, sat deceivingly in the sky.

I looked at my dad.

"I'm sure glad I have several layers on."

I looked towards the sun and then back towards him.

"If you didn't know better, you'd think it would be warmer out."

He smiled. "How many layers do you have on? You don't want to lose the mobility in your arms and shoulders."

"Oh, I just have a sweatshirt and a jacket on over my shirt."

"Okay good," he replied while nodding his head.

He pulled into a parking spot near the clubhouse and stopped the pickup.

"Get the clubs. I'll be back in a minute."

He disappeared around the corner, leaving me to struggle with the golf bags. Mine wasn't so much of a problem. It was his! I was a strong girl for my age and size, but dang! His bag felt like it was full of bricks. For all I know, it was.

As if my dad intentionally timed it, I pulled the bags from the back of the pickup as soon as he came out of the clubhouse.

"Did you get the bags, Cali?"

Proud of my huge accomplishment, I nodded. I wanted to act all tough, you know?

The first few holes were standard for my dad and I. We were actually tied after five holes. Even though I was playing a friendly round of golf with him, I wanted to beat him so badly. I knew things were going my way when I hit the ball behind a giant oak tree and somehow was able to hit around it and place the ball on the green on my next shot.

"What the hell was that?!" he yelled at me.

I proudly shrugged my shoulders. Heck, I have no clue how I made that shot. The momentum was all mine. I dominated my dad the rest of the round. He tried to keep up, but I was overflowing with confidence.

After I tapped my ball in at the 18th hole, he walked over and picked my ball up out of the cup.

"Well Cali, good game. I guess I owe you a donut and milk for beating me, don't I?"

I knew better. Even though I beat him, I knew he was going to buy me a donut and milk no matter what. Even if he had won. He would have come up with some other excuse. Yeah, donuts and milk were in the cards no matter what.

"Nope. You owe me two donuts, pops!" I chirped playfully.

"Well, that sounds like a deal, especially since this is the last time I'm going to lose to you."

I smiled. I knew better though.

25

Springtime Freshmen Year

I just got home from smacking the ball around at the driving range. It was nice to be able to wear short sleeves the majority of the time. I threw my bag into the garage, grabbed a glass of water, and ran up to my room.

As soon as I closed my door to my room, my phone buzzed.

It was a text from Brandy!

Guess what?!

What???

There was a pause which drove me nuts. You don't say "guess what" and then make the person wait!

Jamie is no longer dating Megan!

What!!?? No way?!

This was not the time for a text conversation, so I pressed Brandy's name. I could hear her phone ring on the other side.

As soon as she picked up the phone, she started talking.

She didn't even say hello!

"So get this. I guess she broke up with Megan a few weeks ago. Guess who she was seen going out with?"

"Who?" I asked.

"Are you sitting down?"

My cousin was such a drama queen.

"Yes, I'm sitting down," I responded as I rolled my eyes. I wasn't actually sitting down.

"Jeremy! She is hanging out with Jeremy!"

"Wait, what?!" Truly in shock, I sat down on my bed.

"Yeah, can you believe it?"

"I'll give this relationship about a week before Jeremy gets tired of her. She's not for him."

There was silence on the other end.

"You think?!"

"Yep, she's a skank!"

For some reason I was aggravated. I'm not sure if I was mad at Brandy or Jamie or Megan. I just know I was upset.

"Listen, my dad is calling me," though he wasn't. "I have to go."

"Okay cuz, I love you."

"Love you too."

I hung up the phone and began to cry. I felt alone and confused.

26

Springtime Freshmen Year

A couple of days later, I was sitting in class. I looked to my right and noticed Jamie was done with her class work.

"Geeze," I said, "I didn't realize class was almost over."

She smiled weakly, but didn't say anything.

"So… I heard you and Jeremy are dating?"

She looked away and then back at me, but managed to refrain from making much eye contact.

"Where did you hear that from?"

"C'mon Jamie, you know how this school is!"

She ruffled her right hand through her hair.

She was never much of a talker. Which partly explains her short response.

"Yeah, I guess."

I hate to admit it, but I was kind of jealous of her. Though she had her faults, she was one of the prettier girls in the school. She had a killer figure and her hair was just down right beautiful.

"Well, he's a great guy. I'm happy for you."

She smiled.

"Thanks. I appreciate it."

For about a minute there was silence. I didn't usually talk to her, so this was new territory and it was kind of awkward.

The students in class began to pick up their bags, which always signaled the bell was about to ring.

"Hey…" Jamie said, finally looking at me. "I didn't mean to get in the way between you and Megan."

I didn't know what to say, so I said the first thing that came to my mind.

"Don't worry about it. It was for the best."

With that, I gathered my stuff and went to my next class.

The following Monday, I sauntered into my first period class. My weekend was typical. I pretended to work on homework and golfed. Nothing too exciting.

About a minute before the bell rang, Jamie walked into the room and sat down a couple of desks behind me. As much as I wanted to ask her about her weekend and her date with Jeremy, I waited. The class was going to start shortly after all.

As our teacher finished up her lesson, I looked back and noticed Jamie wasn't talking to anyone. She really didn't have any friends. I also couldn't help but notice Megan was in the far corner of the room sitting by herself.

"Hey Jamie, how did your date go with Jeremy?"

She looked at me without responding.

"Why do you care?"

"Not good, huh?" figuring that was where she was heading.

She smiled.

"Nope *dear*, it went well."

"Oh … cool. Glad it went well."

She squinted her eyes.

"What about you? Have you been on any more dates lately?"

"Nope, I haven't."

"Huh," she responded.

"Yeah, besides, I've been busy with golf."

"I bet you have been," she replied.

I didn't quite know what she meant, so I figured I'd let it slide.

"Well have a good day, Jamie."

As soon as I said her name, the bell rang. It was time to move to our next class.

27

Springtime Freshmen Year

As the school year was coming to a close, the baseball team was winning games like crazy. Julio and a few other seniors were guiding the team through the state tournament. As for me, I was playing my best golf to date. It was pretty awesome. As April came to an end, I was in the top spot in the region.

I was slightly nervous the morning of the region tournament. Out of the thirty-six who participated, only the top four would move on to state. Since I was ranked number one in the region, I was slated to tee off last with three other girls. I had beaten all of them before, but this was different. As I approached the tee box for the first hole, I noticed the leaderboard. The scores were not that daunting.

What tickled me the most were the amount of fans that showed up. I could probably have counted the number of fans that came to cheer for me and the other girls from Franklin High School on two hands. It was mostly parents, but there were a few guys my age there. Those guys were the unlucky few that were lassoed into coming. I actually felt sorry for them. I would've thought watching paint dry would've been more fun, but kudos to them for supporting their girlfriends.

I looked at Leslie, one of the girls I was golfing with.

"Looks like a big crowd is here today."

She looked at me as if I was nuts.

The first several holes were fairly tight between me and the others in my group. Leslie Schmit from Carbondale was a sophomore and the reigning region champ. She actually finished in the top ten in the state tournament her freshman year. I was the number one seed because I had actually beaten her that spring.

Like dueling banjos, she and I went back and forth. When she had a good shot, I had a poor one and when I had a good shot, she had a poor one. As we made our way down the fairway of the 8th hole out of the 18, Leslie came up alongside me. She actually surprised me to a small degree.

"You're looking good, Cali."

"Thanks, Leslie. So are you."

"Nah, it's just a matter of time before your shot takes over. You're looking crisp."

I looked at her in disbelief. I didn't know what to say. Here was the returning region champ nearly conceding to me she was going to lose. Was she just trying to psych me out? OH SHIT!

Somewhat surprised, I slowed down. I looked ahead and saw my ball on the green near the flag. Any nervousness I may have had fluttered away. I walked up to the green and looked around. To my surprise, none of the other balls were on the green. The other three were nestled in the longer grass just off green.

"Great shot!"

I looked up and Leslie was standing over her ball shaking her head and smiling.

I smiled back.

The 8th hole marked the beginning of the end for all of the other golfers. I quietly pulled away. I won the region tournament. Like me, Leslie also advanced to the state tournament.

Not long after I arrived home, my phone buzzed from an incoming text. It was Brandy!

The Baseball team is going to Sectionals!!!!

Awesome! I'm going to State as well!

Yeah, the school was slightly more excited about the baseball team than my achievements. Let's just say I was used to it.

The week flew by as I prepared for the state tournament. Each day after school I went out to the driving range. It was free of charge, at least for one more week because I was playing for the school. The deeper the week went, the more confident I felt. Finally, Thursday arrived. Like the super supportive dad he was, he took Thursday and Friday off and drove me up to Springfield. My coach came up Thursday once school was over.

As soon as we arrived at the hotel on Thursday, we checked into our rooms. I laid down on my bed because I was tired. Even though I was tired, I was slightly restless. I was a little nervous, even though I didn't want to admit it.

The next morning I woke up ready to go. I threw on my khaki pants and blue polo. The blue wasn't my first choice, but it was a shirt the school provided. The weather was perfect for a day of golf! The sun was out and the temperature reached the mid 60s.

The first morning went splendidly well. I started off in the middle of the pack, but as the morning went on I noticed my name slowly creep up the scoreboard. By the 12th hole, I was in the top 10. Even though I was excited, I reminded myself to remain calm. Eventually I worked my way to the top six with just two holes left. I squandered that on the 18th hole when I hit a huge oak tree just off the fairway. Damn tree!

Leslie was ahead of me by one stroke. The next day we were paired together. I was torn. Part of me was excited to be paired with her, the other part of me was not so excited.

Like the day before, the sun was out and the temperature was amazing. My start time was mid- morning since I was near the top of the leaderboard. While I was at the driving range, I heard a voice yell my name. I turned around, and to my surprise, it was Leslie.

I stopped what I was doing and gave her a hug.

"I see we're paired together again."

She nodded and smiled.

"Yep, it looks that way."

She paused.

"What do you think of the competition?"

"Oh, it's tough."

She laughed.

"Yeah it is. Well just keep doing your thing and you'll be okay."

"Thanks, I appreciate it."

Out of the corner of my eye I noticed my dad and my coach walking towards me.

"Are you ready to go?" my dad asked.

I nodded my head. "I think."

"Well just go out there and do the best you can," replied my team coach.

My coach, Jim Watson, was typical for most high school golf coaches. Even though he played golf, he didn't do much coaching. That was left to our personal coaches or, in my case, my dad. From time to time he would comment on something I did wrong with my hips or wrists in relation to my swing, but overall he stayed out of my way.

Leslie and I remained tied through the first several holes. I didn't glance at the leaderboard until the 8th hole. To my frustration, I didn't gain on the leaders.

By the 12th hole, Leslie and I moved up two slots. She was now in 4th and I was in 5th place.

"Looks like we need to keep doing our thing," she whispered to me as we walked towards the 13th hole.

I wasn't sure what to say.

I was never much of a talker when I competed on the golf course. Not even with my dad, so the apparent lack of communication with Leslie was typical. She didn't know that though and chances are she thought I was a stuck up bitch. At the end of the day, I was trying to beat her... so it really didn't matter what she thought of me.

As we approached the 16th tee box, I looked up and noticed we had moved up the leaderboard. Ole Leslie was now in 2nd and I was in 3rd place. I glanced in Leslie's direction. I wondered if she had noticed the score change. By the look on her face, she had.

Leslie quietly stepped up to her ball on the 16th tee. With one fluid swing, she pounded the ball down the middle of the fairway.

"Nice shot."

She smiled back at me.

"Thanks, it's your turn now."

My ball flew off the tee like a rocket. It finally came to a stop ten yards past Leslie's ball.

"Crap girl, good hit. Had I known you were going to hit it that well, I wouldn't have said anything."

I smiled.

Even though we both tapped our ball in on par, neither one of us gained any ground on the top golfer.

On the 16th hole, with just two holes remaining, Leslie lined up for her tee shot. She took two practice swings. She stood over her ball and paused while taking a deep breath. Leslie went into her back swing and then followed through.

TING!

Her ball flew off the tee and, at first, it looked really good. Then I heard Leslie mutter "shit" just loud enough for me to hear. Loud swearing was always frowned upon at the golf course.

I watched her ball slowly drift into a sea of oak and pine trees.

The last thing I wanted to do was what she just did. So, I took a deep breath before approaching the tee box. I put my tee into the ground and set my ball on top like you would a cherry on a sundae.

I stepped back and took a few practice swings myself.

TING!

My ball bounced off the tee and flew through the air. It eventually rolled to a stop 175 yards away in the middle of the fair way. Excited, I pumped my right fist.

The rest of the hole went well for me, and even though she started off rough, Leslie had decent second and third shots. I was able to tap my ball in one stroke ahead of her, which allowed me to tie her.

I approached the 17th hole quite energized! I couldn't believe it. My tee shot on the 17th hole was maybe one of the worst I ever had. The swing totally stunk. My ball went only 100 yards down the fairway. Of course, Leslie's tee shot came to a stop 175 yards away. I dropped my head in disgust.

"Hey, keep your head up. You're playing great," she whispered.

Though I didn't respond, I appreciated the words of encouragement. After the 17th hole, I dropped to 5th place with only 1 hole left. By the end of the 18th hole, Leslie remained in 2nd place.

I sat in the dining area with my dad and watched the remaining groups finish their rounds. I ate my sandwich in disgust.

"Don't forget, you're only a freshman. Keep at it. I can

see major improvement out of you everytime you play."

Even though my dad's words of encouragement didn't mean much to me at the time, a few days later they did.

With my season done, I took a few days off from my golfing routine. The baseball team was in the sectional finals and there didn't seem to be an end in sight. Like many of the other students at Franklin, I was more than happy to cheer on the baseball team as they advanced to the state playoffs.

28

Summer After the Freshman Year

Well, the baseball team wound up winning State. My dad was tired from the long school year, so he didn't take me to the State championship. Even after I stomped my feet and slammed my bedroom door. Instead, we sat in our lawn chairs in the back yard and listened to the games while we sipped on some iced tea.

When the game winning hit was made, my dad and I jumped up and down excitedly for the team and for the town. In small towns like Franklin, the sports teams don't only represent themselves but also represent the community. It was pretty awesome to hear some of the guys I went to school with interviewed on the radio as well.

At one point the announcers were interviewing Julio.

My dad looked at me and smiled.

"Mark my word. He's going places."

He must have known something I didn't, because he was drafted in the first round that same week by the San Francisco Giants.

In his younger years, my dad coached with Coach Wilson, which is one of the reasons why they were such good friends. He never told me or went into much detail about why he stopped coaching, so I never asked.

The night after the team won State, Coach Wilson and his wife came over to our house for steaks. School was out and a summer full of golf was about to begin.

I continued to steadily improve my golf game. Without having to prod me very much, my dad continued to make sure I did pushups and lift weights. Sometimes I stood in front of the mirror and flexed. I loved looking at my stomach as well. It became a sense of pride for me. As much as I didn't want to admit it, lifting weights and doing my pushups were paying off. My ball was traveling farther than ever before. It wasn't much to the average observer, but I could certainly tell a difference.

Every few nights I would quietly walk over to Brandy's house or she would come over to mine. Brandy and Kyle had remained together for close to a year. The word had crept out amongst some circles that I was more interested in girls than boys. It still didn't stop some of the guys from pursuing me.

I'll never forget the evening Brandy called me.

"So Cali, I have a question."

"What is it?"

"The other night Kyle was asking me if you're into girls or guys."

"What did you say?"

"Well, I said I thought you liked boys. Why?" She paused. "I guess word is out you like girls too? What should I say?"

Silence fell upon us.

"Cali, are you there?"

"Yeah, I'm here," I replied. "You know... don't say anything. Just let them think what they wanna think. Besides, I'm not sure who I'm interested in."

She laughed. "Okay, sweetie."

After we hung up, I went to bed. That conversation had worn me out.

July 4th weekend snuck up on me. It's funny how we always seemed to look forward to summer break, but once it arrived, it always seemed to fly by. I rolled over and opened my eyes. I had no desire to peel myself out of bed. The previous few days the temperature had been scorching and humidity was through the roof.

Like my dad, I had a knack for waking up early.

"Hey Cali, how was your workout?" my dad asked as he took a sip from his coffee mug.

"Oh, it was good," I said as I wiped the sweat off my forehead.

"Cali, can you sit down for a moment. We need to talk."

I immediately thought I was in trouble.

My dad smiled, which put me slightly at ease.

"Relax, Cali. It's nothing."

He patiently waited for me to sit.

"I've been thinking. I have watched you improve your golf game and I feel we need to hire a personal golf coach to put you over the top. What do you think?"

At first I didn't know what to say.

"Why? I enjoy golfing with you."

He continued.

"This won't keep us from golfing together or going to the driving range together. I just think you have so much potential and it's time for you to get some real coaching."

I didn't respond.

"There's a good coach up in Carbondale. He would want to work with you at least 2 to 3 times a week."

"What would it cost?"

"Don't worry about that. I just need to know if you would be committed to this adventure."

I looked away and pondered my dad's offer.

"I'm in," I said with my eyes as large as saucers.

"Good, because your first session is Monday."

He gathered his coffee cup and plate, which held his toast.

"Wait, what?"

"Yep, I have already paid for your first few sessions."

He grinned at me like an evil cat.

"What if I had said I didn't want a coach?"

"Did you? Nope. I knew you were going to say yes."

My dad walked out of the kitchen and left me in the kitchen by myself. I looked around. Shit, Monday was only two days away. There goes my summer.

29

Mid Summer Before the Sophomore Year

My dad's pickup zoomed down the highway towards Carbondale. I didn't know what to expect from my first meeting with my new coach, so I was quite nervous. What would he look like? How old would he be? Was he nice or would he be mean? These were all questions that raced through my head.

Finally, after a thirty minute car ride, we arrived at the golf course. I had only golfed at the Carbondale National Golf Course a couple of times. Each time I did, I walked away amazed with the beauty and the challenge the course offered.

I looked around for someone that looked like a coach. Several guys were walking to or from their pickups, but they were all carrying a golf bag, so I quickly ruled them out. Finally! At the far end of the driving range stood a tall well built man who looked super old! That must be him!

I wasn't quite sure what to do, so I let my dad lead the way. After what seemed to be an eternity, we finally made it to the end of the driving range where my new coach was waiting.

"Are you Mr. Hank Brown?" my dad asked as he reached out with his hand.

"Yes I am. You must be Jim. Call me Hank."

Their hands met in a polite firm handshake. I, on the other

hand, still lingered behind my dad.

My dad stepped to the side and guided me towards Hank with his right hand.

"Hank, this is my daughter, Cali."

I was impressed with his handshake. It was firm and quick. Nothing is worse than that guy who doesn't know when to let go of your hand.

"Well hello Cali. It's so nice to meet you."

His voice was deep, but not too deep, and very distinguishable. Maybe because he spent his younger years smoking?

He paused for a moment. His shades, which rested on his hat, flashed in the sunlight as he squinted from the bright sun.

"I want you to call me Hank or Coach, okay?" He said sternly.

"Yes, sir." I replied shyly.

I was overwhelmed and nervous. Looking back, I don't know why I was so nervous.

He stepped to the side and with his left hand he guided me towards an area he had set up for us to practice.

"I wanna see your swing. Go ahead and get out your five iron."

I pulled out my five iron and prepared to hit the ball off the ground.

"What are you doing?" he asked me sternly.

It wasn't five minutes in and I was already botching things up. Crap!

"You're going to stretch, right?" he asked. "Take about five to ten minutes to stretch your legs, hips, and back. The power is in the swing."

As I stretched, he mumbled and sang to himself. A couple of times I overheard him repeat "Yep, the power is from the stretching."

The dude even walked in circles as I stretched. As soon as he sat down on one of the benches behind the driving range, I stood up. I was finished and ready to take a whack at the ball.

I wiped off my shorts as I scanned the area for my dad. I was comforted when I saw him in the distance. He was sitting alone on one of the benches.

"You ready?"

"Yes, sir," I replied politely.

"Sounds good. Let me see you hit a few." He tipped over the large sized golf bucket he had in front of me. It must have contained close to thirty golf balls.

Again I replied, "yes, sir."

I still didn't know what to think of this guy. I figured he was good at what he did otherwise my dad wouldn't have hired him.

I put one of the balls on the green mat used for hitting off of, stepped back, and gripped my five iron. I took a deep breath and gathered my thoughts.

DING!

The ball flew 100 yards away. I looked at him somewhat unsure of myself. I was pleased with the hit. I just didn't know what he thought.

"Do that again," he grunted as he flipped me another ball.

I repeated my procedure and again I hit the ball close to 100 yards. I couldn't tell if he was disappointed or impressed.

He bent over and picked up a golf club he had brought.

"I want you to hit another one," he muttered as he flipped me the ball.

Again, I went through the process. The ball came to a stop near the 125 yard mark.

"Nice hit, but I want you to try moving your front foot towards me just a few inches."

As awkward as it looked, I figured he knew what he was talking about. I whacked the ball pretty good, but to my surprise, the ball drifted a little to the left approximately 100 yards out.

Perplexed, I looked at him, not sure what to think.

He smiled.

"So sue me, I wanted you to hook the ball." He flipped

me another ball.

For the next 45 minutes he worked with me on my swing, suggesting minor tweaks here and there where he saw the need. Finally, we emptied the bucket.

He motioned me to the ground.

"I want you to give me three sets of ten pushups."

After rifling through my pushups, he instructed me to complete three sets of twenty sit ups. Thank God both were nothing new to me.

My dad had wandered over to where I was working out.

"So how did it go?"

"Oh, she was just fine. She has a nice swing." There was a pause. "Thursday, right?"

I turned my head left to right while the two talked. It probably looked like my head was on a swivel.

My dad wrapped his arm around me.

"We will be here Thursday."

Though I was still trying to figure him out, I was no longer nervous.

Hank looked at me.

"Thursday we will work on our drives and chip shots. Today I just wanted to see your swing and to get a feel for things." He paused. "You need to hit the driving range at least two times a week outside of our sessions, okay?"

I gladly nodded my head.

"Well Hank, we'll see you Thursday. We need to head home before her mom gets to worrying about her."

Hank belted out a loud booming laugh. I laughed as well, even though I wasn't sure if I was laughing at my dad or the discovery of my Coach's laugh.

My dad and I walked towards his pickup.

"Hey Dad, can we stop for a donut?"

He threw his right arm around my shoulders.

"I don't know why not. We just need to let your mom know."

Excited, I smiled. Mainly for the opportunity to chow down on a donut with my dad, but I was also excited about working with my new coach.

30

End of Summer Before Sophomore Year

Between my lessons and golf outings with my dad, the summer flew by. I couldn't believe my sophomore year of high school was only a few weeks away! The town of Franklin was it's same ole boring self, which was probably a good thing because it kept me on track and out of trouble. To my surprise, Jamie and Jeremy continued to date through the summer.

Almost every Friday night Brandy and I got together, unless she and Kyle met up. At times, Jeremy and Jamie would join us. Of course, I was glad to see Jeremy. He was a good guy. Yeah, he was a great catcher, but he was more than that. I was thankful Brandy, Kyle, and I had welcomed him into our small group. Jamie, on the other hand, could have stayed away and I would've been just fine. She was, afterall, partly to blame for my breakup with Megan. Though, looking back, I'm glad it happened sooner than later.

I slowly gained trust in my golf coach. We often spent three nights a week out on the driving range. Then on Saturdays we'd generally go golfing. Sometimes one of his friends would join us. I always enjoyed it when my dad tagged along. He was my dad after all. The other guys who joined us were always impressed with my golf game. Nevermind I beat them most of the time. Yeah, most of those guys never joined us again. They probably couldn't handle losing to a teenage girl. It was amazing how many said it was the worst golf outing they have had in a long time. Imagine that!

It had been a long day on the driving range. Though the temperature was cooler than normal, a few beads of sweat ran down my face and onto the ground. My arms were shiny from the sweat and my hands were slicker than snot.

I was nearly finished with my bucket of balls when Hank looked at me and smiled.

"So, you don't have anything planned this weekend, do you?"

I looked at him. I was a little perplexed because I figured it was our weekend to golf together.

"No, why?" as I shrugged my shoulders.

"Well, we aren't golfing here this weekend."

"Oh, okay," I replied. Though, truth be told, I was a little disappointed.

"Yeah, we're traveling to Nashville for a tournament."

I looked at him in disbelief. I think he could tell I was in shock and curious about the event. I was speechless after all. ME! Speechless!?

"Let's finish up our practice and then I'll give you more details." He paused. "You know your dad already knows about it." The smile on his face was priceless.

I stared at him for a few seconds in disbelief. Practice sped by. My ability to concentrate was rather challenged.

Eventually my dad sauntered up behind us. I always wondered where he hung out. I knew he was near, but I just never knew where.

"Did you tell Cali about Saturday?" My dad asked.

"Yes I did and she looked at me like I had three eyes. I'm not quite sure how to take that." Hank replied jokingly.

I looked at my dad for answers. I was curious about this road trip to Nashville they had kept from me.

My dad looked at Hank and then me.

"We have entered you into a pretty solid tournament. We'll be leaving around noon on Friday so we can arrive in Nashville by dinner."

"Do you think I'm good enough?" I asked him.

My dad opened his mouth as if he was going to talk, but was immediately interrupted by Hank.

"We're having none of that. Of course you're good enough. Hell, I wouldn't be working with you otherwise -- pay or no pay. Is that clear?"

"Yes, sir," I replied as if my tail was between my legs.

The little doubt I may have had quickly disappeared.

"I'm excited!" I told my dad as we walked towards the car.

He looked at me and smiled.

"You will be fine. I'm proud of you."

The night before the big trip, I laid my clothes out onto

my bed. The whole time Brandy sat on my bed and grinned.

"What's up with you?" I asked curiously.

"Oh nothing, just in a good mood."

I smiled. "Uh huh," I muttered.

"What? A girl can't be happy?"

As hard as she tried to hide her smile, it wouldn't come off her face.

"Finally!"

I pounded my clothes into my mini suitcase. Who knew dressing for a two day tournament could be so challenging.

I looked up after finally zipping my bag shut.

"I know, you're such a sucker for Kyle."

"I am, but you want to hear something terrible?"

She lowered her voice as if she had some super-secret. It may have been, but it humored me because I was the only one in the room.

"Is it terrible to say if I wasn't dating Kyle, I'd be so hot for Jeremy?" Her eyes twinkled.

I looked at her in subtle confusion.

"No, it's not bad. Just don't be a bitch and act on it. Kyle really likes you. Besides, Jeremy's dating Jamie."

We started laughing after I mentioned Jamie. Nothing against Jamie, neither I nor Brandy thought she was the right match for him.

I looked at Brandy.

"Well, I need to get to bed. It's going to be a long weekend."

My dad appeared at the door. He looked at his watch, looked at me, then looked at his watch again. Subtle hints were never a point of emphasis with my mom and dad.

Brandy smiled.

"Well, good night cuz, I love you."

"I love you too."

We blew each other kisses as she left my room.

The next morning I woke up, had a good workout, and dragged myself to school. School was the last thing on my mind. I had bigger fish to fry.

I was sitting in my class pretending to be diligently working when a loud voice boomed over the intercom.

"Mrs. Jones."

"Yes!" my teacher replied.

"Please send Calisa Hays to the front office. She's checking out."

My teacher looked at me and smiled.

"Well, have a good weekend."

I jumped from my seat, gathered my things, and scampered out the door. I didn't even try to hide my excitement.

I sat in the backseat of the pickup and fell in and out of sleep as the two old bulls sat up front and talked about the weather, politics, golf, and a bunch of other topics I had no desire to join in on. There were a few times I pretended not to be listening, but I was fully locked into what they were talking about.

Finally, we reached our destination. It was a hotel outside of Nashville approximately fifteen minutes from the golf course. Not long after we arrived, we convened down in the lobby for dinner. I loved being the center of attention. It usually meant I got to choose where to eat. I chose pizza!

After downing some awesome pizza from one of the local pizza places, my dad drove us back to the hotel. As we finished dinner, my dad and Hank fought over the bill. To my surprise, my dad wound up winning. It wasn't the last time they would fight over the bill, whether it would be for coffee, donuts, dinner, or all of the above. We eventually settled into our separate rooms. Dad and I slept in one room while Hank slept in the other room.

My dad and I were watching a movie on the TV when I sat up and hit the mute button.

"So how good are the girls at this tournament?"

"Well, let me just say you have to be invited to play in this tournament."

"Invited? What do you mean, invited?"

My dad paused for a moment. I'm not sure if it was because of the riveting show we had on or because he was trying to think of the right response. Though quite honestly, I had a feeling he was deep into the show.

"We got the invite in the mail this summer. I guess this tournament hosts the top fifty golfers in the region."

"Huh, imagine that." I said out loud.

I eventually fell asleep, even though the TV was still on. The next morning I woke up and rolled over in my bed and quietly thought to myself about the day ahead of me. I had no idea what to expect from my competition nor did I know what to expect from the golf course.

Not fully awake, I stumbled to the shower. My dad was sitting up in his bed when I came out of the bathroom.

My dad looked at me and smiled.

"Well good morning, Sunshine. Whenever you're ready for breakfast let me know."

Like a bratty teenager, I just growled softly under my breath. I gathered a pair of sweats and a t-shirt and went back into the bathroom.

It didn't take long for the three of us to eat our breakfast.

My dad was away grabbing a waffle or two when I looked at Hank.

"How did you sleep last night? I hope it was quieter in your room than mine."

Before he had a chance to respond, my dad rudely joined us.

"So what are you two talking about?" my dad asked.

Hank winked at me.

"Oh, we're just talking about the course. She's curious if there are a lot of trees on it."

I giggled to myself.

As soon as I finished my yogurt and bagel, I sauntered back to my room. I put on my golf clothes and then relaxed for a few minutes. I even found a moment or two to happily scan the weather forecast on my phone. To my excitement, the weather looked quite favorable -- sunny with temperatures in the 80s.

We pulled up to the golf course. The drive from the road to the clubhouse must have been a half mile in length, or so it seemed. On each side of the road stood a row of trees which were perfectly planted and pruned. I was already in awe and I hadn't even stepped out of the car yet!

My dad pulled up to the first spot he came to, which was so like him. Even though I'd be walking all day, I knew a small walk would do me good. I walked around the back of the pickup and pulled my clubs out.

"Are you fine with Hank being your caddy?"

My dad was so sweet the way he asked.

Of course I didn't want to offend my dad, so I shrugged off his question.

"Oh yeah, that's fine."

Hank tugged on my shirt sleeve.

"Let's head on over to the driving range. Your dad will get you signed in."

Slightly overwhelmed, I looked at my dad and then Hank.

"Yes, sir."

Girls near my age were at the driving range, while others practiced chipping and putting the ball on the practice green. Men and women of different ages were scurrying about from one place to another. Many of them were workers at the tournament, or at least appeared to be. Yeah, there was a lot of activity going on.

As my tee time neared, I slowed the pace in between my practice swings. Eventually, we walked over to the putting green. I wanted to make sure I got my practice putts in.

I noticed Hank glanced at his watch.

"Okay Cali, let's get going. Time for you to rock."

"Sounds good."

I tapped Hank's fist with mine.

The walk to the first tee went pretty darn quick. I couldn't get over the size of the crowd hovering around the first tee. It wasn't in the thousands or anything like that, but it was definitely bigger than any crowd I had seen before. Many of them consisted of fathers and mothers with their daughters, which was pretty cool. In the crowd were what looked like coaches from some of the colleges or universities in the region.

I was paired with two other young ladies. I never did get their first names, though I do know their last names were Smith and French. I only knew this from the sign which followed us everywhere that first day by an older gentleman.

From the start everything went amazingly well. Almost every tee shot I hit went down the middle of the fairway. Yeah, I was on fire and my score reflected it. At the same time, the other two couldn't get into a rhythm.

Maybe Hank's favorite phrase "nice and easy" was a good one after all. He kept saying it and I kept on rocking!

That night, after we had a bite to eat, I walked back to the hotel. Even I was quite drained. Walking eighteen holes is great exercise, at least on the days when you're playing well. Had I not been playing well, then walking the course would've felt torturous.

The next morning I woke up tired, but once I jumped into the shower, I was ready to go. We went through the same routine as the day before. If it worked then, why wouldn't it work the next day, right?

I somehow wound up near the top of the leaderboard, which meant I was teeing off in the last group. The wait until my tee time was the biggest torture for me. I was ready to get out there and hit that little white ball.

Well, the good vibes I had the previous day carried over to the next day. The poor girls I was partnered with didn't even have a chance. I remember walking up the final hole with a four shot lead over the next girl.

"Hey Cali, you can smile now."

I looked over and I proudly smiled at Hank. I couldn't believe it. I mean, yeah, I have competed in the regionals at high school, but this was a whole new experience.

"Come on, smile," he repeated.

Appreciative of his support, I looked at him and finally smiled.

"Thanks, Hank."

"Just relax and breathe," Hank whispered as I approached the ball, which was longingly sitting on the green. I took a big breath in and exhaled. The last thing I wanted to do was miss an easy putt, but then again, I was up by several strokes so I could've afforded to miss one. It just wasn't ideal by any stretch of the imagination.

Finally, I softly tapped my ball into the cup. I looked up and tears streamed from my eyes. I looked at Hank who was walking slowly towards me and pumping his fist. To my left I could see my dad quickly walking towards me. I ran up to him and jumped into his arms. All the hard work on the driving range had finally paid off.

"I'm so proud of you, sweetie," my dad whispered in my ear.

"Thanks, Dad. I love you."

"I love you too." he said with a smile.

I looked at Hank. I'm sure I was a mess. My eyes must have been beat red from the tears.

"Good job, Cali."

I lunged forward and threw my arms around him. "Thanks!"

As I walked by a group of people to sign my score card, I noticed a little girl who must have been 5 or 6.

The smile on her face was priceless. She was clapping away and the gap in her smile because of her missing teeth was so freaken cute.

I stopped and knelt down in front of her.

"What's your name?"

"Carolyn," she replied.

It was the cutests thing.

"Well Carolyn, here's my golf ball. It's yours."

I reached into my pocket and pulled out the golf ball I was using.

"Remember, don't let anyone tell you what you can or can't do. Okay?"

She nodded her head and replied, "okay." She then looked up at her parents, smiling.

I stood up and looked at her parents who mouthed "thanks" to me. I probably had the biggest, cheesiest grin on my face.

After the ceremony, we piled into the pickup and began our drive back to southern Illinois. I think I may have grinned the whole way home. By the time we got there, it must have been 11 O'clock. I was quite tired.

What a weekend! Too bad the next morning I had to get up and go to school. Winning a major tournament like the Nashville Invitational made it all worthwhile.

31

Fall Sophomore Year

It was just a few weeks into my sophomore year. I couldn't believe I was no longer just a freshman! That was definitely nice.

I was sitting in my first period class waiting patiently for the bell to ring. I was a little more sore than normal, which is why I remember that morning. I had just started a new workout routine and Hank was working me overtime at the driving range. Not that I was complaining of course. I could see improvement in my golf game.

Seconds before the bell rang, Jamie bound through the door. I couldn't wait for the day she would be tardy. There was a group of guys in the parking lot that liked to do drugs and she notoriously hung out with them much of her freshman year. Once she started to date Jeremy, she didn't hang out with them as much. Brandy and I did see her every once in a while with the group, which bothered us. Not because we had any great concern for her, but because Jeremy was our friend.

I just shook my head when she plopped in her seat.

Our math teacher, on the other hand, took it another direction. Mr. Sampson was quite the hardass. I really didn't like his class, but I laid low so he never seemed to yell at me. Jamie was a different story.

"Nice of you to join us," he muttered.

Jamie didn't reply. I'm sure she didn't want him on her case either.

He stomped around for a few minutes all because Jamie made it to class just before the bell rang. I couldn't help but giggle. She did make it into the room on time after all, so I thought he was being a little dramatic.

"So class," he continued, "remember Monday we have a quiz."

One of the ball players raised their hand.

"Can we retake it if we don't do well on it?"

Mr. Sampson silently looked at him.

I'm sure he had a few words in his head he couldn't say aloud.

The rest of the period went on drama free.

In between the class periods, I was walking towards my next class when I came upon Brandy.

"Hey, what are your plans for the weekend? Do you want to get together tomorrow or Sunday?"

I replied without hesitation. "Sure."

After all, what else would I be doing?

"I do have a test to study for, so maybe tomorrow instead of Sunday."

Brandy flipped her hair to her right side.

"Sounds good! I'll talk to you later I hope."

Just as we were about to finish our conversation, Jeremy came up to us.

"Hey guys, have you seen Jamie?"

Brandy and I looked at each other.

"God I hope not," Brandy replied, which I thought was kind of bitchy.

"Well she was in my class, but I haven't seen her since then."

"Why?" asked Brandy.

"Ohhh … no reason," replied Jeremy.

I looked up at the hallway clock.

"Well kids, I'd love to stay and chat, but I need to get to my next class."

Brandy looked at Jeremy.

"Yeah, so do we. Let's go."

As I turned to walk to my class, I stopped and looked in the opposite direction. I couldn't help but notice how cute Brandy and Jeremy looked walking together.

32

Fall Sophomore Year

After a weekend of "studying," playing golf, and hanging out with Brandy, it was math test time. Shit, I hated tests.

Like clockwork, Jamie walked into class just before the bell rang. She seemed a little more besheveled than normal, but otherwise nothing out of the ordinary. It was Monday after all and most of us looked a little rough.

I giggled as I looked around the room. Yeah, the expressions on my classmates' faces said it all. None of us were going to do well on the impending test, except for those few that were among the top of the class. They made me sick. Upon reflection, I know many of them busted their butts for good grades, but at the time, I blindly thought it came easy to them.

Our teacher was one of those that never sat down. He constantly walked around the room. He definitely got his steps in.

Finally, I finished the test and just in time. I glanced around the room and many of us had the same expression. One of dismay and grief.

When the class bell rang, we all stood up like we were called to attention, gathered our bags, and made our way towards the door like bugs to a light. Unlike the rest of us, Jamie was moving a lot slower and somewhat awkwardly.

159

I wasn't more than half way down the hall when I heard a loud bang and a couple of students started to scream and panic. I turned around and noticed a girl on the floor, convulsing, and throwing up everywhere. It was really sick and very scary.

Like me, most of the students around me were frozen in the spot they were standing. I didn't know what to do. None of us did.

Out of nowhere, Brandy ran around the corner and a few teachers rushed by me.

I soon noticed it was Jamie who was on the floor. I couldn't believe it. Vomit was in her hair, her eyes went to the back of her head several times, and her body wouldn't stop shaking. I had never seen anything like this before and to be honest I never wanted to see it again.

Just about the time I realized it was Jamie, one of the teachers pointed at me.

"Go to the office and call for help."

I looked to my left and then to my right.

Shit! I couldn't remember where the office was. My mind went blank!

Once my mind came to, I went into a full sprint. Of course, a few oblivious students got in my way and slowed me down. I and a few others did our best to push the other students to the side as we rushed towards the office.

While I was passing students I heard a number of people

yell, "call the ambulance!"

Needless to say, it was a frantic few minutes!

For some screwy reason, I wanted to find Jeremy. I figured he would be easy to spot since he was the only black kid in the halls, but my mind was in such a rush. I didn't even notice that I ran by him.

Once I reached the office, I pushed open the main door.

"Call an ambulance!" I yelled.

The principal rushed by me with a walkie talkie in his hand.

The secretaries looked at me. One of them was already holding a phone.

"It's Jamie. She's in the hallway. She's throwing up!" I screamed.

I didn't even know Jamie's last name, so I'm sure a few of the ladies in the front office wondered who Jamie was.

I didn't know we had so many teachers. They all seemed to come out of the woodwork. Some tried to move students on, others tried to assist Coach Wilson, while others just stood there like statues.

As much as I wanted to help, I didn't know what more to do, so I just stood back. Thankfully I found Tommy, one of my friends and a baseball player.

"What happened?" he asked.

"Oh, Jamie got sick," I replied.

"Is she okay?" he asked.

I looked at him with my mouth open. That was the dumbest question I ever did hear.

Finally the ambulance with it's whirring sirens appeared in the parking lot. Four guys in blue uniforms rushed through the main doors with a stretcher.

I looked at Tommy.

"Well let's get to class."

He nodded his head. "I hope she's okay."

"Yeah, no shit." I replied.

As I walked by her to get to my next class, I couldn't get over how bad she looked. The floor was covered in vomit, as was her hair, and her shirt was damp from the mix of vomit and sweat.

Later that day I was walking to one of my classes when I noticed Jeremy.

"Hey man, are you okay?" I asked.

He silently looked at me and just nodded his head.

I looked at him with my hand out.

"I'll be praying for her."

I lightly grabbed his hand and caressed it.

"Thanks," he muttered.

I passed him and ventured to my next class. I tried to forget what I saw, but I couldn't get it out of my head.

The school day finally came to a close. It couldn't have

come fast enough either.

That night I was lying in bed. Just drained from the day. The vision of Jamie having a drug overdose really took a lot out of me.

Just as I was about to fall asleep my phone buzzed.

It was Brandy

How r u Cali?

I'm okay, how r u?

Drained

There was a pause. She may have been like me and falling alseep.

I hope Jamie is okay

She didn't immediately respond.

Yeah...maybe Jeremy will finally realize she's not for him

Though I didn't disagree, I didn't think it was the time. I always thought Jamie was a bitch and not the right person for

Jeremy, but he had to decide that. That was not our decision. Besides, Franklin wasn't the most accepting town to people like Jeremy and Jamie for very different reasons.

Well, see you tmorrow Cuz

33

Fall Sophomore Year

A couple of days later I was walking to my next class when I saw Jeremy somberly walking by himself.

Outside of Jamie, he really didn't have a lot of friends. If you had asked him, he probably would have called Brandy and Kyle friends, but that may have been it. It must have been tough attending an all white, mostly racist school. I never asked him, but I'm sure he would have said it wasn't easy. Even though we didn't talk much to each other, I thought he was a great guy and a good person to know. I definitely considered him a friend.

"Hey Jeremy, wait up!"

Jeremy turned and acknowledged me with a smile and a slight wave.

"What's up, Cali?"

Before I answered him, I embraced him with a big hug.

"How are you doing, you big stud?" I asked playfully.

"I'm okay," he responded while also chuckling.

I was glad to see him smile.

"So, how's Jamie doing?"

Jeremy took a breath.

"She's okay. I talked to her yesterday. From what I understand, she'll be in there another day or so…" There was another pause. "She'll be going through rehab, or at least having to attend a group once a week."

"Cool."

I know that was a dumb answer in restrospect.

"So, when will she be coming back to school?"

"Not until January," he immediately responded.

"Oh yea, why's that?"

He shrugged his shoulders. "I don't know. I haven't asked her that."

I smiled. "Makes sense. Well listen, I need to get to class. Hang in there, bud."

I gave him another big hug.

"Thanks Cali… and thanks for everything."

"Oh, no worries. Have a great day."

After hugging him one last time, I walked to my next class.

I looked back at Jeremy as I walked away. I couldn't help but smile.

34

Winter Sophomore Year

It was the Friday immediately following Thanksgiving. I was in my room reading when I heard a knock at the door.

"Cali, can we come in?"

I closed the book I was reading and sat up.

"Yep."

My dad slowly opened the door. Behind him was my mom.

"Hey guys, what's up?"

Mom sat down at the edge of the bed, while my dad continued to stand.

"Mom and I were thinking. How would you like to go to Florida during your Christmas break?"

"What!?" I asked as the question sunk in.

My mom and dad looked at each other. They both had grins on their face.

"Yeah, we've been talking and we thought it would be fun."

"Could we go golfing?"

My dad belted out a laugh. "Of course!"

"So, wait. You'd only go if you could golf?" my mom asked confusingly.

I grinned. That was my only response.

Several weeks later, the three of us landed in Orlando. Unlike most families who fly to Orlando, we weren't going to stay at Disney.

Even though this wasn't my first flight, it sure seemed like it was. I actually shook with excitement as our plane landed.

I looked at my mom and dad and smiled.

"It just looks warmer out there."

They glanced at each other and then at me.

"That's because it is warmer," my mom said with a grin.

We eventually got off the plane and walked towards the baggage claim. I was worried my clubs wouldn't be there. Thankfully they were. I all but jumped up and down when I saw a huge pink travel golf bag appear on the baggage belt.

The next day, after a day of golfing with my dad, we sat down for dinner. My mom rode along with my dad in the golf cart while we golfed. She wasn't much of a golfer. After wolfing down some pizza, I looked at my parents.

"Guys, I'm moving here once I graduate from high school."

"You are, huh? And just how do you think that will happen, dear?" my mom asked. Unlike my dad, she never really saw me going to college on a golf scholarship. Dad, on the other hand, was another story.

"I'll make a deal with you, if you find a school you like down here and they offer you a golf scholarship, even if it's just a small one, we'll do whatever we can on our end. Deal?"

My face widened with an enthusiastic grin.

"Dad, that's a deal!"

Even though it was time to go, after a week of sun and golf, I definitely didn't want to leave the Sunshine State.

Several days after I returned to Franklin, I called Hank. I was already motivated to play golf in college, if not the pros. The thought of moving where it was warm excited me the most!

"Hey Hank, what Florida schools are good ones to attend for golf?"

He paused.

"Why Florida?"

I paused. I thought that was a stupid question.

"Well, there are a lot of courses down there and it's warmer than here." I replied.

"Well, there are a lot of good schools in Florida. Have you thought about colleges in Arizona or California?"

"No. Why? Should I?"

"Well Cali, you're a darn good golfer. Don't sell yourself short. It's definitely smart to move to a warmer state, but keep your options open."

I knew I was good, but it was nice to hear, especially from my coach. His validation was appreciated. Though only a sophomore in school, I was ready to start my search.

I wanted to get out of Franklin as soon as possible.

I hung up the phone and tossed it to the side. A smile raced across my face. Yep, I made the determination right then and there I was bound for greener pastures. Where? I wasn't sure, but I knew I was and golf would be my ticket.

35

Winter Sophomore Year

It was the first day after Christmas break and I was in my seat waiting patiently for the first period to start. I remembered Jeremy saying something about Jamie returning to school, but I had forgotten. As much as I didn't want to admit it, she looked amazing. I always thought she was pretty, but damn.

She walked across the room and gave our teacher her schedule. She then turned and walked in my direction.

"Hey Jamie, how are you?"

She sat in the seat next to me.

After putting her books on her desk and her purse around her seat, she looked at me.

"I'm fine, thanks."

"How was your Christmas?"

She took a deep breath. I didn't quite know what that meant, but I had a feeling I was bothering her.

"Mine was fine. How was yours?" she then asked shyly.

"Ehh, no complaints," I replied with a smile. "Sure would rather be at home than solving for X, that's for sure."

She didn't immediately reply.

"So have I missed much since I was here last?"

I couldn't help but laugh.

"C'mon Jamie, this is Franklin High School."

The bell rang soon after I said that. Through much of the period I pretended to think about solving for X or Y, but I couldn't wrap my head around Jamie. She seemed fresher.

As soon as the bell rang, everyone gathered their belongings and began to go to their next class. I, on the other hand, stayed back. I wanted to say hello to Tommy, who I hadn't talked to since leaving for Christmas break.

"Hey Cali, how are you doing?" he asked when he noticed me looking at him.

"I'm doing well. Did you have a good break?"

"Yeah, I did. I slept a lot….What about you?"

"I did, thanks. Sure beats being here," I replied.

He looked ahead, presumingly to make sure Jamie had left the room.

"Well, I see she's back."

"Yep, it looks that way. Anyways, I just wanted to say hey to you. It's been a while."

"Yeah it has...Sometime we need to get together?"

I looked at him somewhat shocked. Tommy wanted to hang out sometime? Huh, I sure wasn't expecting that!

36

Spring Sophomore Year

Spring eventually came. Yep, it was time for the spring sports to rock. I was so excited for another golf season and all my baseball friends were equally excited for another year. I know Tommy was. He wouldn't stop talking about it in class.

Though her free time was mainly spent with Kyle, Brandy and I got together whenever we had the chance. It was the Friday before their first baseball game.

"Hey Jeremy! Hey Jamie!" I yelled.

They were rounding the corner of the hall, coincidently where Jamie had her overdose. They both stopped. Jeremy smiled while Jamie gave me a "you're a bitch" look. I didn't blame her. I wasn't necessarily the nicest person to her, but I had been trying.

I greeted him with a fist bump.

"Are you guys ready for your first game next week, Jer?"

It wasn't the most girly thing, but then again, I wasn't the most girly girl.

"Oh yeah," he said with a wide smile.

"Nice!" I paused for a moment. "Is Kyle pitching?"

"Yep, I believe so." He paused. "I think Kory will come in around the fourth inning, though Coach hasn't really said."

As I talked to Jeremy, I could feel Jamie staring me down.

"Are you going to the game Tuesday?" She asked me.

To this day I wish I knew what my facial expression was, but I truly can't remember. I know she surprised me.

"Nah, I don't think I'll be able to make the game. I have golf practice in Carbondale."

"Well if you change your mind, I'll probably be at the game," she added shyly.

"What do you mean you'll probably be at the game?" Jeremy asked jokingly.

Jamie nudged him playfully.

"Well guys, I have to run. The bell is going to ring shortly."

The weekend zipped by. Besides working out and reading in my room, I didn't do much. I wish I would've found time to spend with Brandy and Kyle, but you can't live life with regrets.

The boys on the baseball team were quite excited as Tuesday finally rolled around. Hey, I get it. There is nothing like being excited for something, especially something you love to do. Speaking of which, I greeted Hank as he waited for me at our typical spot on the driving range.

"You ready, Cali?" he asked me as he rubbed his hands together.

"Sure am, Coach," I replied with a smile as I began to stretch.

Practiced breezed by. Like any practice, Hank would often say to me, "keep your head down, watch your hands, BREATH." It was nice to be out on the driving range with Hank again.

It was between 6 and 6:30 when practice finally came to a close. Like every other practice, Hank had me stretch and then do several sets of pushups and sit-ups.

I was walking to my dad's pickup when I felt my phone vibrate.

"That's weird," I muttered to my dad.

Before he had a chance to reply back, I clicked on my phone.

"Hello? What's up Brandy?"

On the other end was Brandy, though I wouldn't have known it except for the caller id. There was silence except for screams in the background and I could hear people crying.

"Brandy...Brandy, what's wrong!?"

There was silence.

"Brandy...Brandy...Are you okay!?"

"Kyle's dead!" She replied hysterically.

"Wait, what?"

"Kyle's dead! A ball hit him in the head and he's dead!" She screamed hysterically.

I dropped to the ground. The phone fell out of my hand as I cried uncontrollably. Consumed with agony, I lost all understanding of my surroundings. I couldn't even feel the presence of my dad and Hank kneeling around me.

"Are you okay, dear?" my dad asked while rubbing my back.

I tried to speak, but words couldn't come out of my mouth. I realized I didn't hang up the phone, so I reached over and grabbed it.

"Brandy, are you still there?"

The other end was dead. "No!" I bellowed.

Tears flooded down my face.

"Take me home, Daddy."

"Okay, okay," he whispered to me. "Let's get you home."

Hank gathered my clubs as my dad lifted me to my feet.

"Let's get you home, Cali."

The drive back to Franklin was long and agonizing. I tried to call Brandy, but she didn't answer.

As we approached Franklin, I looked at my dad. Tears were still in my eyes.

"Can we go over to Brandy's?"

"Sure," he said softly. He looked at me and rubbed my arm as reassuringly as possible. As much as I appreciated my dad's comforting support, I just wanted to curl up into a ball and cry.

After a number of lefts and rights, we finally reached Brandy's house. As our car came to a stop, I swung open the door and jumped out.

In a full sprint, I ran towards the back of the house where I figured she would be. Brandy was hunched over in one of the chairs and crying. Her mom was sitting on the couch next to her.

She looked up and noticed me running towards her. Her upper cheeks were black from the mascara and her eyes were red.

"Cali, Cali, Cali!" she repeated as she threw her arms around me.

"I'm so sorry," I whispered. As if a dam had been built up inside her, she exploded into tears, many of which ran onto my shirt as they dripped from her face.

For several minutes we stood and embraced each other. She continued to cry which made me cry.

Finally, I sat her down as I continued to hold her.

"How in the world did the ball kill him?" She whimpered.

"Shh... shh... shh..." I repeated. The last thing I wanted her to think about was Kyle's death.

"Why,? Why now?" she muttered tearfully.

I couldn't answer that question. The best I could do was cry with her, which of course, I did. I just wished I would've taken up Jamie's invite and gone to the game. I didn't know it was going to be Kyle's last game. But... I have learned you can't live with regrets. They'll eat you up.

37

Spring Sophomore Year

The next month was a rough one. The baseball team was stinking it up and Brandy was definitely lost. Heck, she had been dating Kyle for the last 2 years. I'm just glad she had supportive friends like Jeremy and I.

One evening, I was studying in my room when I heard a soft knock on my bedroom door.

"Who is it?"

"It's Brandy. Can I come in?"

"Sure," I said as I slid my books to the edge of the bed.

She walked in and plopped down on the bed. It was the first time I had seen her smile in such a long time.

Before I had a chance to ask "what gives" ole Brandy started talking. Her chipper attitude threw me a little.

"So, what are your thoughts about Jeremy?"

A devilish grin ran across my face.

"What do you mean Brandy, by 'what are my thoughts about him?'"

"Am I a bitch if I want to get him to break up with Jamie to date me?"

I belted out a laugh. "Um, yeah."

She opened her mouth to defend herself, but I interrupted her.

"You may be a bitch, but I definitely wouldn't blame you for trying. I think you would be better for him than Jamie. I mean, she has grown on me and I haven't been fair to her in the past, but come on Brandy, you two are a nice fit."

Her smile widened.

I continued. "Do you want to be one of those girls though? Besides has it even been a month since Kyle's..." I stopped at Kyle's name.

I could tell her brain was working overtime. "Huh," she said out loud while looking off to her right.

"What are you thinking?" I asked. "I mean, go after him. You need a good guy in your life. I just know it sucks to be dumped. Remember, it's only been a month also."

"Yeah, I know, and I do miss Kyle." she paused. "Sometimes I just sit outside alone and confused."

She paused again.

"Well, I'm going to run. Get back to your studying, nerd."

"Geeze, leaving so soon? Okay, talk to you later Cuz!"

After she left, I decided I would make an appearance at one of the games. I had been meaning to attend a game. The following Saturday morning I woke up and got in my workout. After working up a sweat, I showered, and then went to Vienna with my dad. I had every desire to go with Brandy, but she had left for the game before I had a chance to ride with her. Besides, my dad had been wanting to go to a game.

The game was less than exciting, especially since Franklin lost. During much of the game, Jamie didn't seem to be herself. She seemed rather depressed. I wanted to ask her if she was okay, but she didn't seem to want to talk. After the game, I watched the players somberly board the bus.

"Well girls, my dad and I are going to head out."

Brandy leaned over and gave me a hug.

"Talk to you later, Cuz," she added playfully.

After acknowledging the other girls, I looked up to wave goodbye to Jamie. To my surprise, she was gone.

"Huh, that's strange," I mumbled.

Brandy, who was in the middle of a conversation with one of the other girls, looked at me strangely.

"What's strange?"

With my head I motioned towards the bleachers.

"Jamie… She's gone. I was hoping to say goodbye."

Baffled, I looked at Brandy and the other girls.

"Did she say goodbye to you guys?"

"No," everyone responded in tandem.

"Well, no matter. I guess I'll see her Monday in class."

I gave Brandy one more hug and made my way to my dad's pickup. As I walked towards my dad's truck, I thought about Jamie. I couldn't help but feel bad for her. As hard as she tried, she just couldn't find her niche at Franklin High School.

38

Spring Sophomore Year

The next morning I woke up. The house was quiet like most Sundays. On the days we went golfing it was a little more hectic. To my surprise, my phone dinged. I picked it up and looked to see who was texting me.

It was Brandy.

Call me when you get a chance!

Worried, I tapped on her number and called her immediately.

"Hey Brandy, what's up?"

"Yeah...umm," she paused for a moment. "Jamie killed herself last night."

"What? No way! Are you kidding me?" I muttered as tears began to run down my face.

"Nope...I guess she shot herself in the head."

Brandy's voice sounded a mile away though it was just on the other end of the line.

In shock, I reached for one of the kitchen chairs so I could sit down. I wasn't as smooth as I wanted to be, which brought attention to my dad who was in the living room watching the news.

He appeared around the corner.

"Are you okay?"

I looked up at him with tears in my eyes as I shook my head.

He walked over and sat down next to me. I worked hard to keep from sobbing. My lips quivered.

I looked at my dad. Tears streamed down my face. He reached for a napkin and handed it to me.

"Jamie killed herself last night."

Somberly, my dad rubbed my arm.

I hung up the phone, oblivious to what Brandy was actually saying, and laid my head down on the table.

"No, no, no," I cried.

I could feel my dad's hand run across my back while he quietly sat next to me.

"Dad, why am I such a bitch?"

"Shhh... Shhh..." he whispered.

I sat up and looked at him. My eyes were red and welled up from the tears.

"I could've been so much nicer to her. But I wasn't."

My dad paused for a moment.

"Well then, use this to better yourself, Cali."

I wiped my eyes with the back of my hands.

"That won't change the fact Jamie's dead."

"Ohh that's true, but the greatest way to show respect to

someone in life or death is to pay remembrance to them.”

My lips quivered.

“Thanks, Daddy,” I whimpered as I laid my head on his shoulder.

“You don't need to thank me, hun,” he whispered.

“Can we go out to the course today? I want to get out and hit some balls.”

“Sure, I have nothing going on today, though we probably want to ask mom first.”

“C'mon Dad, you know she'll let us.” I responded with a small smile as I wiped away the remaining tears.

“True. our mom is pretty understanding.” He paused. “You never know what kind of chores she may have in store for us.”

A couple hours later, the cool breeze felt good on my face as I lined up to hit a practice ball off the tee. To my surprise, Coach Wilson appeared.

I threw my club down, ran over to him, and wrapped my arms around him.

“Coach,” I squealed.

“Hey Cali.”

“Are you here to hit some balls as well,” I playfully asked.

“Yes I am, but I know it's fruitless to try and compete with you.”

For the next few hours we all escaped from the real world.

A few times I looked up and smiled as I watched my dad or Coach Wilson take a hack at their golf ball. Don't get me wrong, they were always good players, but I started to notice a difference between my play and theirs and that was gratifying!

At one point I thought about Jamie. Yeah she did drugs, yeah she was rough around the edges, but of all the girls in Franklin, she was one of the nicer ones. Sad how that works.

I began to cry.

39

Late Spring Sophomore Year

Much to my aggravation, I was in a funk the rest of the school year. Thankfully, my dad, Coach Wilson, and Hank did their best to keep me focused. Hank definitely didn't allow me to feel pity for myself. He wanted me to grieve, but every time I stepped onto the driving range or the golf course he pushed me to be better. Much to my disappointment, my sophomore season at Franklin High School ended poorly as far as golfing went. The competition was pretty solid in our region and I didn't make it out of the regionals. It didn't help that I played some of my worst golf either and Leslie played solid golf as always.

The Saturday prior to my last week of school, I went golfing with my dad and Hank. There was a golf course in Marion that Hank wanted me to play. Of course, I was all in.

It was still early in the morning when the sun peeked over the horizon which created an orangish glow. The sporadic clouds enhanced the colors even more. It was absolutely beautiful.

The first few holes were a bit of a challenge, but I was able to get that little white ball into the hole on par. We didn't walk. Instead, we rode golf carts. Otherwise, our shoes would've been soaked because the ground was so dewy.

When we reached the 7th hole, we piled out of our respective golf carts. Dad drove by himself while I rode with Hank. The hole was a par 3, meaning the ball should be in the hole in 3 shots. Up by the tee box, we looked down towards the green since we were on a major hill. The hole was about 175 yards away from where we were standing, but it seemed much closer.

Both my dad and Hank hit their balls. My tee box was just a few yards ahead of them, so we didn't need to get into the cart to get to my tee box.

Prior to my tee shot, Hank called me over to where he was standing.

"Hey Cali, come here for a moment, will you?"

Hank had a smile on his face.

I walked over to him and stood by his side.

"Look at that, Cali. Isn't it just beautiful?"

I stood next to him, speechless. I wasn't sure what he was referring to. I listened for the birds, but I didn't hear any, so it wasn't that.

He wrapped his arm around my shoulder.

"Do you see that oak tree down there behind the flag?"

I looked towards the hole. Behind the flag, marking the hole, stood a huge broad oak tree.

"Yes, sir."

"Well, I have been golfing here for the last twenty years

and every year I come to this course that tree seems to be taller and broader than the previous year. It doesn't matter how harsh the winter is or how strong a summer storm has been. That tree has been a beacon of strength."

He paused as he looked at me.

"Cali, you're a damn good golfer." He paused. "You're going to run into storms along the way, which are going to rock you."

He paused while he took a breath.

I began to tear up.

"I want you to imagine yourself as that oak -- strong and beautiful. If you do that, nothing is going to stop you in this world. Nothing."

I stood next to him, speechless.

"Promise me you will be like that oak."

He pointed with his club down towards the tree.

I nodded my head. Choked up, I found it hard to talk. For some reason, I was slightly embarrassed to be tearing up in front of him.

"Alright then, let's par this hole," he said as he cheerfully laughed.

I mustered up a smile.

"Sounds good to me."

I approached my tee box, set my ball up on my tee, and went into my backswing.

TING.